A
LAURA MARLIN
MYSTERY

THE SECRET
OF SUPERNATURAL
CREEK

Praise for the Laura Marlin Mysteries

'. . . clear, warm-hearted storytelling'
The Times

'. . . a cut above. St John's best work of
children's storytelling to date'
The Sunday Times

'. . . it demands to be read – and so it should be . . .
this simply ticks all the right boxes. The first in a
warmly-awaited series'
Daily Mail

'It has enough intrigue to keep independent readers
engaged, and is a pleasure to read aloud to the under 10s'
Daily Telegraph

'Another cracking adventure . . . a page-turner with plenty
of action and twists to keep young readers engaged'
Telegraph

'A refreshing . . . mystery adventure with a traditional,
almost Blytonesque feel, but a thoroughly modern
and tenacious heroine'
Bookseller

'As always, Laura Marlin makes for a redoubtable heroine
who can teach the professionals a thing or two about
mystery solving'
Booktrust

'One of the best series around for younger readers
keeps getting better'
Bookbag

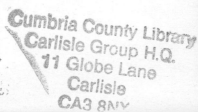

Also by Lauren St John

LAURA MARLIN MYSTERIES

Dead Man's Cove
Kidnap in the Caribbean
Kentucky Thriller
Rendezvous in Russia

THE WHITE GIRAFFE SERIES

The White Giraffe
Dolphin Song
The Last Leopard
The Elephant's Tale
Operation Rhino

THE ONE DOLLAR HORSE TRILOGY

The One Dollar Horse
Race the Wind
Fire Storm

The Glory
The Snow Angel

A
LAURA MARLIN
MYSTERY

THE SECRET OF SUPERNATURAL CREEK

Lauren St John

Illustrated by David Dean

Orion
Children's Books

ORION CHILDREN'S BOOKS

First published in Great Britain in 2017
by Hodder and Stoughton

1 3 5 7 9 10 8 6 4 2

Text © Lauren St John 2017
Illustrations © David Dean 2017

The moral rights of the author and illustrator have been asserted.

A CIP catalogue record for this book
is available from the British Library.

ISBN 978 1 5101 0264 4

Printed and bound in Great Britain
by Clays Ltd, St Ives plc

The paper and board used in this book are from well-managed forests
and other responsible sources.

Orion Children's Books
An imprint of
Hachette Children's Group
Part of Hodder and Stoughton
Carmelite House
50 Victoria Embankment
London EC4Y 0DZ

An Hachette UK Company
www.hachette.co.uk

www.hachettechildrens.co.uk

For my godson, Matis Matarise,
in the hope that he keeps reading and following his dreams . . .

'I am the Tree.
You are Me. With the Land and the Sea.
We are One Not Three.'

Kevin Gilbert, Indigenous Australian Author & Activist

~ PROLOGUE ~

'FLYING DOCTOR, THIS IS KATHERINE CLINIC. WE HAVE A CODE ONE EMERGENCY.'

NURSE OLIVIA WARD braced herself. In its century of operation Australia's Royal Flying Doctors Service had dealt with many unusual medical crises, but recent events at the Katherine Gorge had taken weirdness to a whole new level. On a scale of 1–10, Livvy Ward rated them a 12.

She blamed the heat. When the Outback sun broiled their brains, even sensible people with triple-digit IQs became as barmy as bandicoots. University professors set off on twenty-kilometre hikes without water, hats or phones. Grey Nomads (pensioners in campervans) roared across deserts and along bone-shaking Kakadu roads like teenagers on a joyride, then were surprised when they had heart attacks at the wheel.

These, however, were common occurrences. The goings-on at the Katherine Gorge were not. At the RFDS base station in Alice Springs, normally discreet doctors and nurses joked about them beside the watercooler.

'Did you hear the one about the woman who was watching the sunset at the Katherine Gorge? She fell off a cliff after seeing a wallaby walk on water.'

'Was it religious?' Dr Gordon had asked before bursting into rude laughter.

Days later, a fisherman had to be taken for a 'psych' evaluation after crashing his truck following a night-time encounter with 'demonic piranhas' with red teeth.

Never mind that there *were* no piranhas in Australia.

And an entire family had wrecked their canoes and suffered an array of ghastly injuries trying to escape in the darkness from a shoal of 'monster fish with eyes like headlamps'.

So when the Katherine Community Clinic called with a Code One emergency at 7.45 p.m. on the hottest night of the year, Livvy Ward steeled herself for more silliness. Instead she heard the words that struck fear into the heart of every man, woman and child in the Northern Territory: 'CROC ATTACK!'

The details were sickeningly familiar: *Forty-seven-year-old male tourist. Severe trauma to right hand. Heavy blood loss.*

Livvy rapidly initiated the process that would dispatch

an aero medical team within minutes. She couldn't help wondering whether the attack was an unfortunate case of being in the wrong place at the wrong time or if the tourist had courted disaster. It never failed to amaze her how many people tried to imitate the late, great wildlife presenter Steve Irwin by wrestling crocodiles, only to find the croc wrestling them instead.

The Northern Territory was a place of extremes. Boiling deserts and lush tropical wildernesses. Raging floods and leaping wildfires. Cuddly possums and savage or lethally poisonous reptiles. The only thing any RFDS team crew knew for certain was to expect the unexpected. Their onboard medical kit reflected that. Depending on the emergency, they carried vacuum mats, head collars, ventilator machines, chest tubes, heart monitors, infusion pumps, snake and spider antivenom, drugs, dressings, drips and bandages.

'The ambulance will meet the plane at the airstrip,' said the community nurse at the clinic near the Katherine Gorge, a majestic natural wonder carved through Northern Territory wilderness. 'There'll be someone on the ground checking for stray emus, camels and kangaroos before it lands.'

'And bush turkeys,' Livvy reminded her. 'If a couple of those decide to party on the runway, our crew will be the ones in need of rescue, not the patient.'

She was about to sign off when the nurse said: 'One more thing. Either the patient suffered a blow to the head or he's missing a couple of kangaroos in the top paddock, if you know what I mean. You might want to pack a safety blanket and have him assessed by a mental health professional once he's out of surgery. His description of the croc – it was a little spooky.'

Something in her tone sent a chill up Livvy's spine. 'How spooky?'

~ 1 ~

ST IVES, CORNWALL, UNITED KINGDOM. ONE WEEK LATER.

'**DO YOU BELIEVE** in aliens?' Laura Marlin asked her uncle over a boiled egg and Marmite soldiers.

Calvin Redfern poured himself another coffee. It was brewed the way he liked it, more rocket fuel than breakfast beverage. 'Aliens? Yes, I do.'

Laura stared. Former Chief Inspector Redfern was a legendary seeker of truth. He dealt only in fact. That's why *Future Science* magazine was propped against the toast rack. Once he'd been Scotland's most decorated detective. After the death of his wife, he'd quit the force and moved to St Ives and these days, so far as the outside world was concerned, he was an ordinary fisheries inspector in and around Cornwall.

Only Laura and her best friend, Tariq, knew the vital role he'd played in the Secret Intelligence Service's (MI6) decade-long operation to bring the Straight As to justice. Laura was still struggling to take in that the gang's key players were safely behind bars, their reign of terror over.

Nearly six months had passed since Edward Ambrose Lucas, then Deputy Prime Minister of the UK, had been sensationally unmasked as the Straight As' shadowy leader. The news that criminal masterminds had infiltrated the corridors of power at such a high level had caused shock waves around the world. Even now, half a year later, feverish media interest surrounded Mr A's story. His upcoming court case began in less than a week. Television crews from as far afield as New Zealand and Alaska were descending on London in the hope of attending it. The newspapers were calling it the 'Trial of the Decade'.

Until then, Ed Lucas was being held in solitary confinement under heavy guard within the razor-wired walls of a maximum-security prison.

Logically, Laura knew that Mr A could never harm her again. Even so, he stalked her nightmares and ruined her daydreams. She'd be doing something utterly unrelated, such as painting a parrot for an art project or walking Skye, her three-legged Siberian husky, on Porthmeor Beach, when all of a sudden she'd feel his arm clamp around her like an iron bar. The classroom or beach would melt away and she'd be back in St Petersburg, being abducted by Ed Lucas on a speedboat.

Only a week ago she'd been gazing in the window of the St Ives Bookseller when the wind teased her nostrils with his peculiar smell. For ages after leaving Russia she'd tried to work out what it reminded her of. Finally she'd figured it out. He smelled of the two faces of money.

Crushed to his chest as he used her as a human shield, Laura had been assaulted by the heady scent of luxury. It was the fragrance of the finest cashmere and silk clothes cut by the best tailors; of the gold and steel watchstrap of his Rolex: of new Italian leather shoes, polished to a mirror gleam.

But his expensive cologne failed to disguise the stench of the laundered money that had paid for it all. Nor did it hide the pong of dirty, sweaty cash clutched in unclean hands; cash won by evil means.

Laura had been unable to get that smell out of her head. After catching a whiff of it on Fore Street, she'd shaken like a jellyfish on a wobble board for twenty minutes. For that reason and so many others, she was counting the hours until she departed on the school trip to Australia. If cuddling koalas didn't take her mind off Mr A and his 'Brotherhood of Monsters', nothing would.

Skye's wet nose nudged her insistently, bringing her back to the present. Discreetly, she slipped him a strip of buttery Marmite toast.

Her uncle opened his mouth to object but she cut him off. 'You're telling me that you, a detective . . .'

'Former detective . . .'

'. . . believe that little green men go round abducting people in flying saucers? Or are aliens huge slimy things with black teeth? Do you think they're going to take over the planet and destroy us in some gruesome way?'

Her uncle was amused. 'Oh, you mean those kind of aliens? No. I don't. But neither do I believe we're alone in the universe.'

Laura cocked her head. 'So who do you think is out there?'

'No idea. Could be something as microscopic as bacteria that, once unleashed on earth, will wipe us out. Could be super-beings who are as handsome as film stars and as saintly as Mother Teresa and are not in the least slimy, pointy-headed or Darth Vader-like.'

He picked up *Future Science*. 'What I do know is that a couple of scientists recently updated the Drake Equation, with intriguing results. Ever heard of Frank Drake? He was the pioneering American astronomer and astrophysicist responsible for the SETI.'

'The Search for Extraterrestrial Intelligence Institute,' said Laura. 'Yes, I've read about it. So you do believe in aliens?'

'Hear me out. In the sixties, Drake attempted to calculate the number of active, extraterrestrial civilisations in our Milky Way galaxy. His equation was clever but there were too many improbables. The new Drake calculation by Adam Frank and Woodruff Sullivan is ingenious. Mathematically, they've proven that what has happened here on earth has been replicated at least ten billion other times in cosmic history.'

He flipped through the magazine until he found the article. 'Here's the equation that shows that the odds of us being the only intelligent species on a habitable planet in the universe are less than one in ten billion trillion.'

'That good?' said Laura.

'Less of the sarcasm, please. Here's the equation. It's a simplified version of Drake's original:

$$N_{ast} \times f_{bt}$$

'That's infinitesimally small by the way!'

Laura was unconvinced. Scientists knew a lot but they didn't know everything. They had yet to find a cure for the common cold.

Her uncle tucked *Future Science* into a vacant slot in the toast rack. 'Why are you asking about aliens, anyway? Do *you* believe that there are little green men roaming round Mars, plotting our destruction?'

'No,' said Laura, 'I don't, and a few N plus X equals Cs in a magazine are not going to change my mind. I'm only asking because, yesterday, our teacher showed us a story from last week's *Darwin Examiner*. It's about the Katherine Gorge, where we're going to be camping when we're in the Northern Territory. In a million years, you'll never guess the headline.'

'Uh, "BOXING KANGAROO CROWNED HEAVYWEIGHT CHAMPION OF THE WORLD"?'

Laura laughed. 'Good try but not even close. "ALIEN

CROC FLYING DOC CRASH CAUSED BY UFO."'

Calvin Redfern choked on his coffee. 'You're joking!'

'Nope. And it isn't funny because the Flying Doctor and pilot crash-landed and ended up in hospital themselves. The plane is a wreck. They were responding to an emergency callout late one night. A tourist almost had his hand bitten off by what he described as an "alien" crocodile.'

'What made him think it was an alien croc as opposed to a regular one?'

'It glowed a fluorescent green.'

Her uncle pushed his chair back. 'Oh come on, Laura. Someone is having a lark. Either it's a spoof story or the bitten tourist had overindulged in the local liquor.'

'Yes, but that doesn't explain the UFO. That's what Eden Jackson, the pilot, thinks it was, and she doesn't seem the type to make up stories. She's worked for the Flying Doctors forever and is quite old. About fifty.'

'Ancient,' her uncle said drily.

Laura flushed. 'Sorry, I just meant . . . Anyway, she's highly respected. She told reporters that, as she flew towards Nitmiluk National Park, a blinding white light shot out of nowhere and hovered in the sky right in front of them. While Eden was dealing with that, the cockpit computer system fizzled and died. She had to make an emergency landing in pitch darkness.'

'Did everyone on board survive?'

'Thanks to Eden's fab flying skills, yeah, they did, but the plane was smashed to pieces because some kangaroos got in the way. Apparently, that's a hazard of landing in the Outback: kangaroos, camels and bush turkeys. And emus.'

Her uncle shook his head. 'I knew I should have taken that job with the Australian Federal Police when I was offered it. Investigating alien crocs and UFOs would have been so much more fun than doing battle with failed burglars and the Straight As. What's the doctor's version of events? Is he also claiming they were pursued by a flying saucer?'

'Dr Kelly was napping at the time. He'd been up since dawn with a patient and slept through the whole thing. Not the crash-landing, obviously, but everything else.'

Calvin Redfern snorted. 'Course he did. Wouldn't surprise me if it emerged that Ms Jackson did too. Asleep at the controls of a plane; it's the stuff of nightmares. Where did you put your Australian itinerary, Laura? Are there any excursions in light aircraft or helicopters? No? Just as well because I'd have banned you from going on them. It's disturbing enough that you'll be spending ten days in a country notorious for having ten of the world's most venomous snakes.'

'Tariq says that snakes only bother you if you bother them.'

He smiled. 'Doubtless, the same applies to UFOs. You're travelling to one of the wildest, most remote places on earth. You will have to keep an eye out for creepy-crawlies but I think I can safely guarantee you won't have to worry about aliens. Or fluorescent green crocodiles.'

'Or the Straight As,' added Laura.

'Or the Straight As. In one way or another, you've been through a lot in the year since you moved to St Ives. You're due a proper holiday, Laura. Just relax and enjoy yourself. You deserve it.'

~ 2 ~

MELBOURNE, VICTORIA, AUSTRALIA. ONE WEEK LATER.

'IF THIS IS a dream, please don't wake me up,' said Tariq as he sipped a salted caramel milkshake on sunny St Kilda beach.

Before meeting Laura and Calvin Redfern, and being adopted by a Bengali couple in St Ives, Tariq Miah had spent most of his eleven years working long, backbreaking hours. He'd started life as a quarry slave with his parents in the South Asian country of Bangladesh, smashing rocks and sewing fine tapestries as soon as he was old enough to lift a hammer and thread a needle.

After being orphaned, he'd been taken by traffickers to

the UK and forced again to work for free or starve. Half a year after being rescued, he still savoured every hour of freedom.

Not that his new life was all plain sailing. Being best friends with the finest girl detective in Britain (in Tariq's opinion) came with certain challenges. You had to be a bodyguard, champion puzzle solver, art expert and animal whisperer rolled into one.

In the short time he'd known Laura, Tariq had been kidnapped, half drowned and come close to being incinerated by a volcano. He'd risked life, limb and sanity on numerous other occasions. Still he wouldn't change a day of it. Well, maybe those particular days but none of the rest.

Beside him, the girl who'd got him into most of those scrapes lay stretched out on a candy-striped towel in the sunshine. She was engrossed in a novel about Matt Walker, her favourite detective. Her strawberries and cream milkshake stood forgotten and melting.

Every few pages she paused to scan the beach. Anyone watching would have assumed that she was simply enjoying the scene, but no matter how relaxed Laura appeared she was always alert for trouble. Even on vacation and even with the Straight As securely behind bars, she could not entirely unwind. Behind her shades, she was studying the surfers and sunbathers for inconsistencies, for anything that didn't add up. In Laura's mind, if something seemed too good to be true, it usually was.

She took off her sunglasses and sat up with a yawn. 'What did you say, Tariq? If this is a dream, you don't want to be woken up? I'm surprised you can tell the difference. I'm so jetlagged that if you told me St Kilda beach was a hologram, I'd believe you.'

'It was quite a long journey.'

'Quite?' Another yawn shuddered through her. 'Astronauts get to the moon in less time than it took us to get to Melbourne. If I didn't love Skye, my uncle and St Ives so much, I'd beg the Australians to let me stay forever just so I wouldn't have to travel another thirty-five hours home again.'

'Yes, but it's worth it. Here we are on a beautiful beach with the sun beaming down.'

'Almost as good as Porthmeor Beach in St Ives, five minutes from our front door.'

'Where it's been raining non-stop and blowing a freezing gale for weeks,' Tariq pointed out.

Laura pulled a face. 'Ugh. Don't remind me. The more freezing and hideous it is, the more Skye loves it. I'll miss him but not the early morning walks in the pouring rain.'

She swirled her milkshake and speared a strawberry with the straw. 'Oh, Tariq, you know better than anyone how excited I am to be in Australia. It's been top of my travel wish list ever since I read *The Silver Brumby*. I can't believe that we're here thanks to a free school trip. I keep thinking there must be a catch, like there was when we went to the Caribbean.'

Tariq bounced up to put his cup in a nearby bin and returned to her side. 'Laura, the entire reason your uncle ran a background check on the ex-St Ives Primary pupil who donated the money for it was to set your – *our* –

minds at ease. We know for definite that Bella Taylor is a professor of International Relations in Scotland and does tons of charity work. We know she has children of her own and wanted to give something back to the school that inspired her. Anyone who pays for half of Year Six and three teachers to tour Australia for ten days must have a good heart.'

'You're right,' said Laura. 'There are millions of kind people in the world and Bella Taylor is one of them. I need to be more trusting. I'm going to give up being suspicious the way some people quit chocolate. I'll go cold turkey this very minute.'

She sucked in a breath, counted to sixty and blew it out in a whoosh. 'There, I'm cured. What were you saying before, Tariq? Something about being on a beautiful beach with the sun beaming down. Isn't it heaven? I have to say, I'm loving Melbourne's funky vibe.'

He laughed: 'So am I but I can't wait to be out in the wild. There are over four hundred bird species in the Northern Territory, plus a hundred and fifty mammals and three hundred reptiles. If we're lucky we might see an eastern brown, the second most deadly snake in the world. There are death adders too. They're rare but they're sometimes found hiding under leaves in Nitmiluk National Park where we'll be camping.'

Laura shivered. 'Great. I'll try not to think about that when I'm curled up in my sleeping bag.'

'Snakes don't . . .'

'. . . bother you unless you bother them,' she finished for him. 'Yes, so you keep telling me.'

He grinned. 'Because it's true. Mostly. Saltwater crocodiles are different. They're wary of humans but if they're hungry they'll eat anything and anyone that gets in their way. Did you know that in the NT, there's one croc for every person – around a quarter of a million?'

Laura stood up. 'I do now. Hey, I have an excellent idea! Why don't we stop thinking about all the things that can kill us with one bite and go and paddle in the sea? It's such a glorious day.'

They ran down to the water's edge. The sea was colder than it looked and they stuck to the shallows. Two of their classmates were bravely bodyboarding in wetsuits, watched over by St Ives Primary teaching assistant Paula Robson, a former county swimmer.

Aside from Elspeth Roper, who was reading in a deckchair, most of their classmates were enjoying a game of beach volleyball with Jason Blythe, the Australian teacher who'd met them at Melbourne airport. Mr Blythe would be assisting Paula and their Year 6 teacher, Giles Gillbert, as they toured the country.

Mr Gillbert and Jason Blythe were polar opposites. While Jason Blythe hurled himself after the volleyball as if his life depended upon it, Mr Gillbert anxiously patrolled the beach. He was slathered in sunblock, making his thin white limbs appear even whiter. Beneath a floppy beige hat, his face was shiny with sweat. As Laura watched, he collapsed into a deckchair near Elspeth and mopped himself with a towel.

By contrast, the tanned Jason (Laura found it hard to think of the teacher as Mr Blythe when he barely seemed old enough to shave) bounded tirelessly after the volleyball. He had overlong sun-bleached hair and wore board shorts and a surfer T-shirt. To Mr Gillbert's obvious disapproval, he'd been only fractionally smarter when he met them at the airport.

There was a loud cheer as Jason Blythe performed a spectacular sliding dive to win the game. He bounded up, slapping sand from his shorts and knees. The kids on his team crowded round to high-five him.

Tariq laughed. 'I like him. He's cool. Kind too. He let Roscoe and some of the other boys watch the Everton game on his iPad.'

Laura didn't reply. She wasn't sure what to make of Mr Blythe. He seemed nice but she was always suspicious of adults who tried overly hard to be down-with-the-kids. It was as if they'd never grown up.

The teacher glanced up and caught her staring. He grinned. Laura turned away hastily, joining Tariq in the frothy fringes of the waves. They watched in awe as a kitesurfer used a breaker as a launchpad for a somersault.

A young voice piped up: 'Looks like paradise, doesn't it? You'd never know the dark forces that lurk beneath the surface.'

Laura and Tariq exchanged amused glances. 'Hello, Elspeth,' they said in unison.

Elspeth Roper, eleven going on fifty-five, was dressed in her version of beach casual. Despite the heat, that involved a cardigan. She was clutching a book entitled *When Kings Go Missing: The World's Greatest Unexplained Events &*

Disappearances. In the term she'd been at St Ives Primary, Elspeth had earned a reputation for being obsessed with both history and mysteries so Laura wasn't surprised by her choice of reading matter.

'What dark forces? You mean sharks?'

Elspeth regarded her pityingly. 'Everyone thinks that Australian beaches are a magnet for sharks but it's a myth. Only one or two people a year are killed and a few lose a leg. Meanwhile, about one hundred million sharks are murdered around the world every year by humans. They're the real victims.'

She held up *When Kings Go Missing*. 'The author of this book doesn't believe a great white or any other shark ate Harold Holt, the Australian Prime Minister. That's the number one most famous disappearance in this country. In December 1967 he went for a swim at Cheviot Beach in Portsea, just along the coast from here. One minute he was bobbing happily in the water, next he was gone.'

She lowered her voice. 'Or did he die? That's the sixty million dollar question. His body was never found.'

Tariq was sceptical: 'You're saying that the Australian Prime Minister went for a swim and never came back? How is that even possible? Where were his bodyguards?'

Elspeth shrugged. 'He refused to have any. And there were no lifeguards on the beach. He was with friends but it was high tide and there was a powerful undertow so they stayed close to the shore. Marjorie Gillespie watched him the whole time. The waves were enormous and she was nervous he'd get into trouble. Next thing the sea boiled up around him and he was gone.'

'So he drowned,' said Laura. 'Doesn't sound like much of a mystery to me. That's awful. Poor man.'

Elspeth shook her head. 'It's not that simple. First, he was a strong swimmer and it was one of his favourite bays. Second, he was in a whole heap of political trouble. If it was a simple drowning, why would the Australian government take nearly forty years to hold an inquest to investigate how he died? No, something sinister went on, no doubt about it.'

Laura stifled a giggle. Elspeth's expression was so earnest it was hard not to. She had no difficulty relating to the girl's fondness for mysteries, being more than a bit obsessed with them herself. Unfortunately, Elspeth didn't think about them in the scientific way a detective might. She adored conspiracy theories, the more far-fetched the better.

Her school project on Howard Carter's discovery of Tutankhamen's tomb had featured twenty sensational theories 'proving' that the Egyptian boy king's tomb was cursed. She began by telling them how Carter's canary was gobbled by a cobra and ended by claiming that a mummified hand fulfilled an ancient prophecy by causing fire and flood at a house in the US.

Listening to her presentation had only enhanced Laura's respect for Detective Inspector Matt Walker. No one had better instincts than her fictional hero but Matt backed up intuition with cold, hard forensics. He was interested in evidence, not gossip or superstition.

'Besides sharks, there are rip currents and box jellyfish around here,' Tariq was saying. 'A jellyfish wouldn't have cared that Harold Holt was Prime Minister. They can kill in minutes.

'If he was really unlucky, he might have got tangled up with a blue-ringed octopus. I saw one at close range in the Caribbean and it wasn't fun. They have blue blood, three hearts and enough venom to kill twenty-six people. Then there are sea snakes . . .'

Elspeth waved a hand dismissively. 'The book doesn't mention any of those things. There are three main theories.'

She ticked them off on her fingers. 'One: He'd been spying for the Chinese for decades and was about to be exposed so he was rescued by a Chinese submarine.'

Tariq hooted. 'A *submarine?*'

Elspeth didn't crack a smile. 'Two: He faked his own death and went to live in France or Switzerland, far from his troubles.'

'What's the third?' asked Laura, unable to contain her curiosity.

Elspeth gripped the book as if the truth was as slippery as an eel and could easily escape from its pages. 'The CIA assassinated him . . .'

'A CIA assassination?' cried Jason Blythe, popping up behind them with a foam football under one arm. 'That's a heavy subject for the beach.'

He did a double take when he spotted the title of Elspeth's book. 'Ah, now I see the problem. You couldn't have brought anything more cheerful to read, Elizabeth . . . ? Elspeth, I mean. Apologies, I'm still getting to up to speed with your names.'

He tossed Tariq the football. 'Lighten up, kids. Leave the gloom in England. You're Down Under now. Us Aussies think beaches are for surfing, laughing and tossing shrimp on the barbie. Pizza's good too. That's what I'm buying everyone now. Wanna come along? I'm so starving I could eat a goanna between two slabs of bark.'

SWINGING IN AN egg-shaped rattan chair outside the café, a delicious breeze in her hair, Laura decided that Jason Blythe was right. Fun and sun was the way to go. Her belly full of the best pizza she'd ever eaten in her life, she watched a yacht tack across the bay. The live band was taking a break. Inside the cafe, the TV was playing a Sia concert.

Roscoe and Tariq were swapping football tricks, laughing, trying to be Beckham. Elspeth was still buried in her book. Laura debated whether to go over and chat to her, but it seemed too much like hard work. She and Elspeth had nothing in common. She closed her eyes and drifted off.

Next thing she knew Tariq was shaking her awake. One look at his expression and she scrambled to her feet. They ran into the Sweet Spot café. A red banner was scrolling across the TV screen:

BREAKING NEWS . . . CRIMINAL MASTERMIND IN DARING ESCAPE.

The presenter said crisply: 'The former Deputy Prime Minister of Britain, who has been charged with leading one of the world's most notorious gangs, is tonight on the run after escaping from a maximum-security prison in a helicopter.

'Less than forty-eight hours before Edward Ambrose Lucas was due to stand trial at the Old Bailey in London, he was plucked from the exercise yard by masked men in a black chopper. It's already being described as the most audacious prison break in British history. Investigators allege that Lucas, code-named Mr A, is the mastermind behind the Straight A gang, a criminal empire worth billions.'

The floor swayed beneath Laura's feet. It was as if the cables had snapped in a lift she was riding in and she was hurtling down a shaft with no bottom.

'As a parting insult to the authorities, the helicopter scattered hundreds of playing cards across the prison grounds, every one a Joker, the calling card of the gang. The Straight As have a history of leaving a Joker at the scene of their crimes, or use the card as a warning to future victims. A nationwide manhunt is underway.

'In other news, scientists are warning that the Great Barrier Reef is being devastated by climate change . . .'

Tariq was in shock. 'I don't understand. Your uncle told me that Mr A was being held in solitary confinement for twenty-three hours a day and only let into the yard briefly at night. That prison is a fortress. How could he escape?'

Laura's voice echoed in her own ears. 'That's what the Straight As are best at. Evading alarm systems. Sneaking behind firewalls. Slicing through the steel doors of bank vaults. Ed Lucas will have spent years scheming how to get out of jail if he was ever caught.'

There were goosebumps on Tariq's arms. 'Good thing we're on the other side of the world. He'll be plotting vengeance against everybody who helped bring down the Straight As. People like us.'

The glass doors of the cafe slid open. They snapped round, half expecting Mr A to come storming in like a gunfighter in a Western, but it was only the new teacher.

He threw up his hands. 'I don't believe it. Everyone else is out in the sun, having a ball, and you're indoors watching the idiot box. Guys, guys, guys, this is not the way to experience a new country. What's so riveting that you'd prefer the TV to the beach?'

His gaze fell on the scrolling headline.

'Ah, someone just told me about Mr X, Y, Z or whatever his name is doing a midnight flit from the British nick in a helicopter. He's like the Ned Kelly of London. You've heard of Ned Kelly, haven't you? In the nineteenth century, he and the Kelly gang were legendary outlaws here in the state of Victoria. For years, the police couldn't catch Ned because he was a bushwhacker and knew every creek, crevice and cave in the Wombat Ranges. He outfoxed them every time.

'They won't catch old Ambrose either. He'll be counting his money in Mexico before I can say "Laura-and-Tariq-it's-time-for-you-to-quit-watching-telly-and-come-out-to-play. We're-off-to-the-St-Kilda-Baths-for-a-swim!"'

That made them laugh. Walking through the restaurant, it flashed through Laura's mind that it was the most idiotic thing ever to imagine that a criminal genius like Ed Lucas would factor vengeance against two children into his escape plan, especially when he was being hunted by every police force in the UK.

Tariq was thinking much the same thing. But as he followed Laura and the teacher to the exit, something odd happened. The afternoon sun was shining directly on the beach-facing window of the Sweet Spot. When Laura paused at the glass doors to allow a noisy family to pass, it projected the cafe's logo – a rainbow-hued target – on to the front of her white T-shirt.

For one eerie moment, the bullseye was over her heart.

~ 4 ~

ST GEORGE'S GRAMMAR School enjoyed what travel writers liked to call a 'faded grandeur'. Once it had been the finest school in Melbourne, the kind of place that produced cricket stars and leaders of countries. Sadly, modern sports celebrities and Prime Ministers are seldom the shining examples they were in days gone by and the same was true of St George's.

From a distance, it still commanded awe. It had black and gold wrought-iron gates topped with the school crest: a dragon being held at bay by a knight on a unicorn. Beyond it was a long and winding driveway flanked by five-hundred-year-old oaks. And beyond them were hockey and rugby pitches, athletics tracks and tennis courts, all empty and overgrown now that it was the school holidays.

The main building was Victorian in style and fronted by stately columns. The sun was setting behind it as the coach drew up, throwing the facade into shadow. The windows gleamed black. They reminded Laura of one-way mirrors. It was as if they'd been designed so that those inside could see out but nobody could see in.

Despite that, Laura liked the school as soon as she stepped inside it. Though the furniture had seen better days and the walls were in urgent need of fresh paint, it had character. Oil paintings of cattle stations in the Outback and Aboriginal art-inspired watercolours done by the absent pupils lined the walls.

The dormitories had high ceilings and big, shuttered windows that were thrown open to the evening air. The dusty, eucalyptus smell of gum trees in heat-baked earth floated in, mingled with the tropical fragrance of what Laura later learned was the butterfly bush.

'Some of you look about ready for the cot,' boomed Annette Brooksby, one half of the laidback couple who ran the girls' and boys' boarding houses at St George's. An actress in a previous life, she could have addressed a stadium without a microphone. 'Can't say I'm surprised. It's been hot enough to roast a chook today. From what I hear, you've been flat out like a lizard drinking since you got off the plane. No worries. Cookie's hard at it preparing your tucker. When the gong goes, there'll be barra on the barbie and chargrilled haloumi for the veggos.'

There was a moment of startled silence. Her broad

face creased into a smile. 'Let me guess – you need a translation?'

'Yes, please,' admitted Naomie, who'd recently arrived in St Ives from Cape Town, South Africa. The other sixteen girls in the group nodded.

Mrs Brooksby laughed. 'That was Australian slang for, "Some of you look as if you're ready for bed. It's been hot enough to roast a chicken today and I'm told you've hardly stopped since you got off the plane. Don't fret. Our cook is preparing an early dinner for you. When the gong goes, there'll be barramundi – that's our most popular local fish – on the barbecue, plus haloumi cheese steaks for the vegetarians."'

After she'd gone, best friends Jess and Mia discovered that decades of polishing made the old floors the perfect ice rink for girls in socks. For several mad minutes the dormitory was a whirl of skidding and twirling and at least two unsuccessful attempts at a triple axel.

Meanwhile, Camilla, who was the cleverest girl at St Ives and knew it, was scouring their lodgings for evidence of its previous occupants, finding a broken hockey stick in one cupboard, and a DVD on a racehorse called Phar Lap in another. The doors to both the dormitory and the bathroom could have been props in an Agatha Christie murder mystery.

'Squeak, squeak,' mimicked Camilla, tugging the dorm door back and forth. 'Screeech, sccrreeeech.'

'Don't,' shuddered Izzy, a slight girl with wavy hazelnut hair that reached almost to her bum. She took her pyjamas and wash bag from her suitcase. 'One of the boys told me that St George's is haunted. That's why Mr Gillbert managed to get us accommodation here so cheaply – because the school is desperate for funds. Every time a pupil sees a ghost, they leave.'

Aaliya let out a little shriek. 'Haunted? My mum would never have let me come if she'd known there were ghosts in Australia.'

'Don't be so gullible, Izzy,' snapped Camilla, tossing her chestnut bob in annoyance. 'He was winding you up. That's what boys do.'

Laura, who had the bed beside Izzy's, gave her a sympathetic smile. Camilla was St Ives Primary's star pupil. She had beauty and brains in equal measure but no tolerance for childishness.

'All schools feel creepy during the holidays,' Laura told Izzy once Camilla was out of earshot. 'They're like those villages where everyone has had to flee a volcano and a camera crew comes back years later to find the tables still laid and covered in dust and one lost shoe waiting for someone to put it on.'

Izzy's face crumpled.

Laura rushed to put an arm around her. 'Sorry, that wasn't helpful. Izzy, I promise you don't have to worry about ghosts. No such thing. Forget *Ghostbusters*. The best scientists in the world have tried to prove the existence of spirits and come up with a big fat nothing.'

'But my aunt saw her dead husband mowing the lawn!' cried Izzy. 'No way would she invent something like that. And did you ever hear that story about the Scottish family who had to flee their home because the oven door kept opening by itself and the lights flickered. The police didn't believe them until a couple of constables came and saw it for themselves. Next thing the family's pet Chihuahua was found on top of a two-metre-high hedge. How else could it have got up there unless there was a poltergeist?'

Laura rolled her eyes inwardly. She could think of any number of reasons why a yapping small dog might end up on top of a tall hedge and a poltergeist was not one of them. But she didn't want to be unkind about Izzy's aunt.

'Did your uncle enjoy mowing the lawn?'

'He hated it.'

'Then why,' Laura asked patiently, 'would he choose to do it in the next life, assuming there is one? I don't know about you but when I'm dead, I plan on relaxing. As for the family with the flickering lights, they'd have been better off getting their oven serviced and calling an electrician, not bothering policemen who are supposed to be pursuing real-life criminals.'

Izzy was unsure. 'But how do you explain the levitating Chihuahua?'

Laura was saved from having to answer by the dinner bell. Ghosts and sock-skating contests were forgotten as the girls stampeded downstairs to the dining hall. The boys, who were staying in the school's second building, on the other side of the tennis courts, would join them there.

Laura was the last to leave. Something was gnawing at her. Something beyond the news of Ed Lucas's escape. So much had happened over the past twenty-four hours that it was hard to decide when the feeling first began to niggle at her. She couldn't be sure. She'd been fine when they arrived at the beach. Lying in the sun reading her Matt Walker novel, she'd been chilled out and happy.

Or had she? Throughout the day, she'd also been slightly on edge. Even when she was laughing with Tariq, she'd found herself studying the surfers and sunbathers for any sign that they were not what they seemed.

The door creaked open. In came Paula Robson. The teaching assistant went directly over to Elspeth's bed and picked up *When Kings Go Missing*, which was lying on the pillow. She was about to open it when some sixth sense told her she was not alone. The speed with which she dropped the book and spun round was quite funny.

'Laura, what the devil are you doing up here all alone? Are you deaf or unwell? Did you not hear the bell? You're missing out on a fabulous barbecue. Go down at once. If you don't hurry there'll be nothing left but crumbs.'

~ 5 ~

OUT IN THE smoky quadrangle, night had fallen as suddenly as a blackout curtain. Laura's stomach growled in anticipation as she queued for the haloumi sizzling on the barbecue. Rain was forecast so tables had been laid inside the candlelit dining hall. Mountainous platters of barramundi, chips and Greek salad added to the feast. What St George's lacked in the way of decorators and groundskeepers it clearly made up for in school dinners. The children fell upon the meal as if they hadn't eaten for days.

'English fish and chips is ace but this is supersonic!' declared Kyle.

His twin sister Mia put down her fork. 'How can you be so disloyal to The Dolphin? Mum's been going there for years and you always say they do the best fish and chips in the world.'

Kyle grinned. 'That was before I tried barbecued barramundi.'

'I guess St George's have to get something right,' said Izzy. 'How else are they going to persuade pupils to stay here with the place falling to bits and ghosts in residence?'

'Not that again,' groaned Camilla.

'What is this ghost supposed to look like, Izzy?' asked Aaliya. 'What's it doing at St George's? I thought ghosts preferred castles or stately homes, or ruined cottages in foggy places like Dartmoor.'

'They're not fussy.' This was Zach. 'It's not as if they can do an online search for a rental property.' He deepened his voice. '"Spectre Estate Agency, for all your haunting needs." Besides, it's a well-established fact that they love boarding schools.'

'The best person to speak to is Lee,' Izzy told Aaliya. 'He heard the story from his cousin in Woolloomooloo—'

'That's never a real place!'

''Tis. It's in Sydney. Lee's cousin is friends with a boy whose sister goes to school here.'

'A third-hand ghost story from a boy in Woolloomooloo,' Laura murmured to Tariq. 'Gosh, it must be true.'

Lee, a large, squashy boy with a wicked laugh, was summoned from the far end of the long table.

He recounted the tale with great solemnity, basking in his five minutes of fame. It all began, he said, on the wedding day of a woman who was finally getting married at the age of thirty-one.

'*Finally?*' said Merryn. 'I'm not getting married until I'm at least fifty and maybe never.'

'Shhh,' hissed Izzy.

'The wedding breakfast was held at St George's, right here in this very dining room. Course, it wasn't a school back in the nineteenth century. It was a mansion. When the guests arrived they found a magnificent cake on the table. They were pretty pleased with that but the food just kept coming. There were trays of smoked salmon and cupcakes and hamburgers and caviar and, and . . .'

'Get to the point,' said Camilla. 'Where were the bride and groom?'

'The bride was in her wedding dress. The groom . . .' Lee paused for dramatic effect. 'The groom never showed up. That's right, boys and girls, the poor bride was abandoned at the altar.'

'Jilted, you mean?' said Laura.

'Whatever. When she realised what had happened, she screamed and screamed until the guests ran for their lives. Then she became a recluse for the rest of her days. When she died, they found her skeleton in its wedding dress. The cake was still on the table, covered in dust.'

Aaliya was pale. 'That is the creepiest story I've ever heard.'

Mia had tears in her eyes. 'What a horrible, horrible man. I hope she put his photo up on Facebook to warn any other woman from marrying him.'

'I don't believe they had Facebook in the eighteen-hundreds,' said Camilla. 'But, hey, maybe they had Spookbook, maybe that's how she got her revenge, by coming back from the grave to haunt the man who broke her heart.'

'That's exactly what she does!' Lee was too carried away with the success of his story to be downcast by her sarcasm. 'My cousin says she walks the halls of St George's carrying a slice of cake on a plate.'

Laura gazed round at the enthralled faces of her classmates. With the exception of Camilla and Tariq, all of them were wide-eyed with fascination or horror. Couldn't they see how ridiculous the story was?

Nobody noticed Elspeth listening silently to the whole exchange. She had a habit of blending into the scenery, usually because she was buried in a book and obscured by her reading glasses and pale blonde fringe. When she spoke, several children jumped.

'The jilted bride – was her name Eliza by any chance? Eliza Emily Donnithorne?'

Lee was taken aback. 'I only know her first name. How did you know the rest?'

'*Because,*' Elspeth told him, 'it's her tragic story that supposedly inspired Charles Dickens to write the character of Miss Havisham in *Great Expectations*.'

A strange feeling came over Laura. It was the kind of thing Matt Walker would have said. That was the reason the great detective immersed himself in subjects as varied as ornithology (the study of birds) and etymology (the study of the origins of words and their meanings), to give himself the advantage over his quarry. He specialised in pulling the rug out from under people's feet.

'The art of detection lies in attention to detail,' her uncle once told her. 'If you're dealing with a cunning killer aided by a brilliant lawyer, the line between conviction and a murderer walking free can be as fine as silk thread. You have to be constantly alert for the word or wrong note that gives him or her away.'

Laura was furious with herself. She'd been so busy judging her classmates that she'd missed the clues linking Lee's 'ghost bride' with *Great Expectations*, which she'd read and loved. Elspeth, on the other hand, had listened closely to Lee's story. Like Matt Walker, she hadn't simply read *Great Expectations*, she'd taken the trouble to learn the story behind the book, something that hadn't even occurred to Laura. Those two things had allowed Elspeth to effortlessly connect the dots.

'You'd make a first class detective, Elspeth,' Tariq said warmly.

'Well spotted, Elspeth,' Laura said with as much enthusiasm as she could muster.

Camilla couldn't conceal her glee. 'I told you it was just some boy talking rubbish, Izzy.'

Lee glared at her. 'Are you calling my cousin a liar?'

'The original story is true,' Elspeth said hastily. 'Mostly. There really was an Australian woman who was jilted on her wedding day. She did leave the cake to rot and spent the rest of her life alone with the front door unlocked in case her fiancé ever changed his mind. But it happened in Sydney not here, and as far as I know she's never come back from the dead. Somebody at St George's obviously read the story and decided it would be a laugh to spin a ghost story—'

'Ah, so you've heard about our resident poltergeist!' interrupted Mrs Brooksby with a smile. She put a tray heaped with watermelon on the table. 'Eliza, she's called, so they tell me. In my experience, she's most commonly spotted after midnight feasts, carrying cake. She's not yet paid me a visit but I'm looking forward to it.'

Izzy clapped a hand to her mouth. 'Omigod. There really is a ghost? That's it, we're sleeping with the lights on.'

Mrs Brooksby was unmoved. 'You'll be right, girl. There was a touch of garlic in the salad dressing. That'll ward her off! Or is it garlic that wards off vampires, and horseshoes and wind chimes that ward off ghosts? I can never remember. I can locate a horseshoe if that'll help.

'In any case, I want you all in your cots in precisely forty-five minutes. I don't want to hear anything or anyone go bump in the night – not unless it's a poltergeist delivering the Victoria sponge of my dreams.'

The watermelon was crisp, pink and homegrown but hardly anybody made a move to touch it. The mention of bed had had a hypnotic effect. Within half an hour all except one of them was dead to the world.

If every zombie in Australia had risen from beneath the floorboards and danced around the dormitory, they wouldn't have stirred.

6

'**THE IMPORTANT THING** is not to panic,' said Calvin Redfern over a crackling line from Cornwall. Or maybe it was his voice that was crackly because he hadn't yet had coffee.

He'd been out all night and half the day dealing with an illegal fishing trawler. When he did hear the news about Mr A's escape he called his niece at once, forgetting there was a ten-hour time difference between the UK and Melbourne. Laura had been tossing and turning. She'd seen her phone light up and answered it.

Now she stood on the moonlit balcony outside the common room near her dormitory. The wind was chilly and carried the iron scent of rain. She pulled her fleece robe tighter as she listened.

'Ed Lucas's escape is highly embarrassing for the Government. No expense will be spared in recapturing him. Every force in Britain is on his trail. The Army has been drafted in to watch the ports and you can be sure that the foreign agents and detectives of half a dozen countries are hunting him in the field and online.'

Laura shivered. 'But who helped him? If the Straight As are mostly locked up and Mr A was being watched twenty-four/seven, who arranged the helicopter and knew when he'd be in the yard? One of the prison officers must have been in on it.'

'Not necessarily. The prison's computer system was hacked two days before. The warden reported it to the police but nobody thought to escalate it to the intelligence service. If they had, MI6 would have taken action immediately. They were so focused on his physical security, they forgot about The Cipher.'

'What's The Cipher?'

There was a pause. On the sports fields below, the shadows of the ancient oaks and whispering gum trees danced and swayed, creating a pantomime in silhouette. Her uncle's disembodied voice added to the sense of theatre.

'I'll risk telling you this only because we're on a secure line. The Cipher is a man, although at times he's seemed more phantom than human. We know almost nothing about him except that he's one of the world's most dangerous hackers. Few computer systems are safe from him. My friends at MI6 believe he's the secret weapon that's allowed the Straight As to pull off their biggest crimes.

'Unfortunately, that's all we do know. He's so adept at evading detection that British intelligence agencies have wasted fortunes over the years pursuing him to places like Siberia and Outer Mongolia only to discover that he's hijacked the online identity of a Yak herdsman.'

'Does that mean he can help Ed Lucas get away?' Laura despaired.

'Not if our intelligence agents have anything to do with it. The Cipher might be able to spirit Mr A out of prison or aid him with false documents, but it's much harder to conceal a helicopter. Find that and we'll find the trail. And don't forget Lucas has been front-page news for months. Ninety per cent of the country can identify him on sight. He can run but he can't hide for long. If he so much as sneezes, he'll be back behind bars . . . Hold on a moment, Laura . . . Skye, it's your mistress on the line. Do you want to say hello? No? Too miserable?'

Her uncle returned to the phone. 'He's missing you terribly, Laura. I'm afraid I'm a poor substitute.'

As if to confirm his words, Skye let out a heart-rending howl. Laura fought back tears. She hated leaving him. Yes, there were times when she wished that he wasn't quite so enthusiastic about ten-kilometre walks in Arctic weather, but even on days when she was being dragged along gale-swept cliffs, she loved him with every cell in her body.

After returning from St Petersburg, she'd taken to using him as a pillow. Any time she had a nightmare or couldn't sleep she would lie with her head on his chest. It was more effective than any tranquilliser. Lulled by the rhythm of his powerful husky heart, beating in time with her own, she'd sleep like a baby.

She'd have done anything to have him with her now. 'Give him a hug for me, Uncle Calvin. I miss him so much. Miss you too.'

He cleared his throat. 'St Ives isn't the same without you either, hon . . . Uh, Laura, about this Mr A business – don't let it spoil your trip. I'm as frustrated as you are that this black-hearted villain has once again made a mockery of the justice system, but I'm certain that he'll be back in custody before sundown our time. That's tomorrow morning in Australia. The net is closing swiftly. Until then, I'm glad you're safely on the other side of the world.'

'*You're* not,' fretted Laura. 'You're not safe on the other side of the world. What if Ed Lucas decides to take revenge on *you*?'

He laughed. 'Aren't you forgetting something? I have Skye to take care of me. Nothing and no one is getting past him.'

Back in bed, Laura felt better than she had all day. She'd been pining for Skye. Knowing he had a job to do, that he was guarding her uncle, comforted her. Two minutes later she was sound asleep.

She'd have found it less easy to drift off had she glanced out of the window and seen a dark car creep without lights up the fire access road that bordered the school.

When the driver reached a place where he could see but

not be seen, he turned off the engine. A takeaway double espresso was swallowed in one gulp. He took out a pair of infrared stealth goggles. It was going to be a long night.

7

LAURA CRAWLED UP through layers of sleep to find the irrepressibly chipper face of Annette Brooksby peering down at her.

'Time to get up, you little bludger! You're the only one still in bed. Believe me, you don't want to miss the brekkie Cookie's whipped up for you. Cinnamon French toast, banana and Cocky's Joy. That's golden syrup to you. Cockatoos love it. But only if you're showered and seated in the dining hall in fifteen minutes flat.'

Laura made it in thirteen but was still the last in line for the French toast. She managed half a slice before Mr Gillbert came to chase the stragglers upstairs. The coach had arrived for the day trip to Daylesford and Blackwood and he was anxious to be off.

In the dormitory, Laura scrambled to get ready. Her phone had gone missing. She was positive she'd left it on the bedside table but it was nowhere to be found.

By the time she'd located it under the bed, everyone else was downstairs. The teaching assistant caught her checking her messages. She was desperate for news that Ed Lucas had been arrested and was on his way to a deep, dark dungeon but there was nothing from her uncle.

'Why are you always the last one to do anything, Laura?' Paula demanded. 'You're supposed to be getting on the coach. Are you one of those Pokemon addicts? Am I going to have to confiscate your phone?'

'No, Miss Robson.'

'It's Paula. Have you brushed your teeth?'

'Not yet, Miss Rob–Paula.'

'Get a move on, please. We're leaving in five minutes.'

'Yes, Paula.'

'On second thoughts, I am going to take your phone and I'll collect everyone else's while I'm at it. We can enjoy being in nature without a soundtrack of pings and pop ringtones. Don't scowl like that. You can have it back at the end of the day. It's not a life and death matter. Thanks. Brush your teeth! Now!'

Slapping some toothpaste onto her brush, Laura hurried out thinking unkind thoughts about the teaching assistant. Today of all days she didn't want to be without her phone. Paula Robson had no idea what Mr A was capable of. It could easily be a life and death matter!

The bathroom was as steamy as a sauna and had a chemical smell. Someone had left a hot tap gushing. Laura attempted to turn it off but it was broken. At the next basin, she gave her teeth a speedy polish and rinsed her mouth. But as she went to stand up a wave of dizziness swamped her. She gripped the towel rail for support. It was difficult to focus. The rising mist was making everything blurry.

Outside in the passage a floorboard squeaked. Then the bathroom door slammed shut.

Laura threw down her brush and ran unsteadily to the door. It was locked. She jiggled the handle and tugged but it was immoveable.

'Hey, I'm still in here! Paula, are you there? Can you let me out? The door is stuck.'

Silence.

'Mrs Brooksby? HELP! Someone! Anyone!'

There was no real cause for alarm. As soon as they did a headcount on the bus the teachers would realise she wasn't there. Or Tariq would tell them. They'd return to the dorm to find her. Even so, she felt panicky. If only Miss Robson hadn't taken her phone. She pulled at the door again but it was no use.

Abruptly, the water shut off. A breeze brushed the back of Laura's neck. An image of Eliza, the Ghost Bride, came into her head. She had an irrational fear that if she glanced over her shoulder an ethereal figure would be hovering in mid-air.

The chemical smell intensified. Laura clutched at the door handle, nervous she was going to faint. Beneath her feet, the floor rolled like a yacht riding a swell.

Out of the corner of her eye, she caught a glimmer. Too frightened even to breathe she turned her head. A Joker had appeared on the steamy mirror, drawn by an invisible hand. It was a message that defied time and geography, a message sent across oceans. Its meaning was unmistakable.

Laura Marlin, we are coming for you.

It was the last thing she saw before everything went black.

~ 8 ~

'I'M NOT SAYING you didn't see what you think you did,' Tariq said in a way that suggested that was exactly what he was saying, 'but obviously it was a prank. With Mr A on the loose, it's easy to get paranoid.'

Laura tried not to take his comments personally. In Tariq's position, she'd have questioned what happened too. That's what good detectives did: they probed. They did not merely accept that a shiny stone was a precious gem because that's what it said on the label. They examined it under a magnifying glass; turned it over to see if anything sinister was lurking underneath. They demanded proof.

And there was zero proof that a ghostly hand had been at work at St George's.

It was Mrs Brooksby who'd discovered Laura lying dazed on the bathroom floor. The door had been wide open and any mist had dissipated. There'd been no broken taps; no steamy Jokers on mirrors.

'Just as well,' she said tartly. 'We don't tolerate vandalism at St George's.'

Laura lay with her legs up on two pillows. Mrs Brooksby and Paula were taking it in turns to press damp cloths to her forehead and bring her cups of sweet tea.

The teaching assistant was mortified. 'Laura, I'm so sorry for abandoning you in the dorm and expecting you to make your own way to the coach. I forgot what it's like to be far from home in a strange country. Combine that with a touch of jetlag and it's easy to see how you might have felt overwhelmed.'

'No, Paula, the fault is entirely mine,' insisted Mrs Brooksby. 'Yesterday I made the mistake of bantering with your pupils about the poltergeist that some of our sillier pupils claim to have seen at St George's. I was trying to ease their fears by making light of it, but it must have played on Laura's mind overnight. The power of suggestion, I suppose.'

She stroked Laura's hair. 'Small surprise you flaked out, honey-pie.'

Laura doubted whether Mrs Brooksby would believe her if she said that she no more believed in ghosts today than she did the previous evening. If an evil spirit had tried to frighten her, she was certain it was human. Once she'd recovered she intended to find out who that human was.

'It wasn't that,' she said. 'Maybe it was jetlag. I'm fine now, really I am. My headache's almost gone. *Please* let me go hiking and exploring with the others.'

But the women were resolved that Laura would be doing no adventuring that day. 'The others will be clambering up and down mineshafts and walking in the heat,' Paula told Laura. 'That's the last thing you need after a fainting fit.'

Laura was crushed. When she heard the coach pull out of the drive without her, she felt absolutely wretched. Her first full day in Australia and she'd be spending it cooped up indoors like an invalid. Not only that, but Tariq had doubted her story.

Though she tried to hide it, Paula was disappointed too. She'd been dying to visit the Macedon Ranges and now she'd miss out because she'd be taking care of Laura.

It was kind Annette Brooksby who rescued the situation.

'I don't know about you, Paula, but when I was Laura's age I couldn't bear being left out of the action. In my opinion, she's made an excellent recovery. The colour has returned to her cheeks. I think there's a compromise to be had here. If I lend you my car and GPS, the two of you can take a leisurely tour of Daylesford and Blackwood on your own. How about it? You could stop for lunch at the Garden of St Erth. It even has a connection to Cornwall. Matthew Rogers – he was the stonemason and miner who created the gardens on the site of an old gold reef – named it after his birthplace.'

Ecstatic to have a reprieve, Laura sprang out of bed. The blood rushed to her head and her knees buckled beneath her. The mattress cushioned her crash-landing. The new outing was almost cancelled immediately and she had to work overtime to convince Paula she was fit to leave the dormitory.

'We'll go on one condition,' said the teaching assistant. 'When we get to our picnic spot near Blackwood, you're to sit quietly in the shade with a book. No argument. Nothing strenuous. Don't worry; you won't be stuck with me all day. Your friends will join us for tea and cake later this afternoon.'

She went downstairs to make arrangements, leaving Laura with her phone. 'You can have it for ten minutes. Do call or message your uncle if you wish. I'll see you shortly.'

Laura switched it on and waited impatiently for it to come to life. When her messages finally came through, there was one from her uncle. Her hands shook as she opened it. *Please, please, please let Mr A have been arrested*, she prayed silently.

But there was only a cute photo of Skye and Lottie, her uncle's wolfhound, accompanied by a cryptic text.

Hope u r having fun in the sun. Don't worry about a thing.
All fine & under control. Love from the 3 of us x

All fine and under control? What did that mean? Had Ed Lucas been recaptured? Or had Calvin Redfern left Skye and Lottie with Rowenna, their housekeeper, in order to help Scotland Yard and the SIS hunt down his nemesis? It was a scary thought. With her uncle, anything was possible.

Since he hadn't felt the need to update her, Laura was relieved of the need to update him about the bathroom drama.

Australia is ace! ☼ ☺ 🍦 Going for a picnic in the Macedon Ranges. Luv to you, Skye & Lottie Lxxx

Paula put her head around the door. 'Ready whenever you are, Laura.'

Laura switched off her phone. 'Ready.'

9

THE TROUBLE WITH being a detective, mused Laura as she and Paula strolled through the pretty, historic village of Blackwood, was that the most innocent of settings took on a sinister aspect.

Where a normal person might visit an idyllic English wood in springtime and be enchanted by a carpet of bluebells, Matt Walker only wondered where the bodies were buried.

Ordinary tourists strolled through Provençal or Tuscan villages, delighting in the sun-drenched piazzas, fields of lavender and shop windows stuffed with cheeses and pastries. Sherlock Holmes, Poirot and Miss Marple knew these places to be hotbeds of intrigue. The jolly woman at the *boulangerie* could have a sideline selling fake antiques for exorbitant prices. The handsome young Italian posing for a selfie beside his scooter might be the middleman for a gang of ivory smugglers.

Calvin Redfern had warned Laura that these detective-coloured spectacles – 'the very opposite of rose-tinted glasses' – once on, were impossible to take off.

'Before you know it, you can't see a barn without wondering if there are kidnapped heiresses concealed in the loft. And after a while it becomes impossible to envision any such thing as a vicar, politician or postman who isn't a blackmailer, a psychopath or both.'

'It hasn't done you any harm,' Laura said. 'You're one of the most hopeful people I've ever met.'

His rueful smile reminded her that that hadn't always been the case. He'd changed. Having a niece and a three-legged husky bring laughter and chaos to number 28 Ocean View Terrace had chased the shadows from his strong face. These days he laughed easily and readily. The deep grooves of sadness that had once hugged his mouth had been replaced by crinkles of amusement.

But Laura was not naïve enough to believe that her uncle had moved on from the past without a care. Indirectly, the Straight As had brought about the death of his wife. He would not rest until each and every member of the Brotherhood of Monsters was jailed or six feet under. She suspected he didn't care which.

Paula's voice came to her from a long way away. 'Oh, Laura, this is such a thrill. In the early days of the 1851

Victorian gold rush, these dusty streets were quite literally paved with gold. It's said that one could walk the slopes of Mount Alexander scooping up nuggets with one's bare hands. You can imagine what happened when word of such riches spread. Laura, are you listening? You seem miles away.'

Laura returned to the present with difficulty. 'I'm right here!'

At St Ives Primary, she'd never warmed to the teaching assistant, whose manner usually veered between bored and spiky. But everyone has a passion and history, it turned out, was Paula's.

'Overnight, ships set sail from every corner of the globe, bringing the hopeful, the ruthless and the desperate. Tent cities mushroomed across Victoria. People dreamed of exchanging their rags for silk and champagne, but for most it never happened. They scratched out a living in lawless camps crammed with ruffians greedy with gold fever.'

These were the kind of stories Laura was interested in – the untold ones. She didn't want to hear about the heroes of the gold rush; she wanted to know about the forgotten people, starting with the children. A staggering twelve thousand had slaved on the mines.

'People thought of them as small adults,' explained Paula. 'Girls and boys of your age and younger worked in the sluices alongside men ten times their strength. Some found it a great adventure. There are photos of grubby urchins proudly holding up crumbs of gold. Some even went to makeshift schools.

'But thousands were grossly neglected. The Melbourne Orphan Asylum was overflowing. The life of any gold rush child was unimaginably hard. Winters in Victoria can be brutal as any in England. Basically, kids were either locked up in cramped, Dickensian orphanages, or they worked back-breaking hours in freezing mud and water and slept in tents battered by rain, wind and snow.'

Laura thought guiltily about the times she'd moaned to her uncle that the heating was not hot enough at number 28 Ocean View Terrace. She recalled her cloud-soft duvet, the steaming shower and Rowenna's divine vegetarian dinners. Best of all, she was loved.

'I'm so lucky,' she said.

'You and I both,' agreed Paula. 'But in a way, so were the people who came here dreaming of a better life. Those who survived helped transform Australia from a colony of convicts and misfits into the diverse, rich nation you see today.'

Laura set down her spoon. 'What about the Aboriginal clans who were here before anyone else came? What's their gold rush story?'

'Oh, it impacted them hugely. The new settlers chopped down trees, took over creeks and turned the hills into a sieve of diggings and garbage pits. But there were positives too. The miners brought goods and food to trade, some of which was helpful to local Aboriginal clans. There are numerous accounts of Indigenous people showing the miners where to find water or how to build shelter. They also tracked for them, healed them with traditional medicine and worked as interpreters.'

Her smile was sad. 'Unfortunately, the new settlers had very short memories.'

Having dreaded being alone with Paula for four whole hours, Laura found the morning had flown. Weirdly, she'd had fun.

Except for one thing. Even after they arrived at the tranquil oasis that was the Blackwood Mineral Springs Reserve, she could not rid herself of the sense that she was being watched.

The events of the morning came rushing back and her hands trembled as she took cartons of juice from the ice-packed 'Eskie' cooler box. The demolition drill that had pounded her skull earlier had gone. More than anything, it was the ferocity of the headache she'd suffered that convinced Laura she'd been the victim of foul play.

'You're being watched,' Paula confirmed as Laura counted out plastic beakers for each picnic table. She gestured towards a grassy mound.

Curly yellow feathers bobbed, like petals, behind it. A talon came into view. Then another. One by one a cackle of sulphur-crested cockatoos sidled over the hillock, doing their comical best to pretend they weren't remotely interested in the boxes containing hummingbird cake.

For precisely thirty-six minutes, the cockies brightened Laura's day. Then the skin-crawling sensation of being observed by persons unknown returned.

She was about to admit this to Paula when a sharp crack made her glance up. A plump koala was sitting on a branch, munching eucalyptus leaves. It gazed down at her with solemn dark eyes.

Laura giggled and poked her tongue out it. She resolved to do a better job of being an ordinary tourist. There was a time and a place for detective spectacles and a cloudless blue day in the Blackwood Reserve was not one of them.

10

LAURA WAS RESTLESS. Mia had loaned her a mystery novel but the schoolboy detectives in it were so wooden and inept that her attention kept wandering. What she really wanted to do was go for a walk, but she wasn't allowed to go off on her own. Unfortunately, Paula had fallen asleep reading *When Kings Go Missing*, borrowed from Elspeth. It lay open on the grass, pages ruffling in the breeze.

Laura picked it up. She'd dismissed it as a manual for conspiracy theorists but was soon gripped. In between the lurid accounts of what did or didn't happen to President Kennedy or the Princes in the Tower were some startling facts. At least, the author claimed they were facts.

One entry was about *Picnic at Hanging Rock*, an Australian classic by Joan Lindsay. Coincidentally, it was set near Mount Macedon, the blue-green mountain range visible from where she was sitting.

The plot was intriguing. Three girls from the Appleyard College for Young Ladies disappear in mysterious circumstances while on a day trip. If Matt Walker had been called in to search for them, the outcome, Laura felt, would have been very different. But he wasn't. There was not a competent detective in sight and the situation went from bad to worse quite speedily.

Absorbed in the story, it took Laura a while to notice that the prickling sensation had returned to her limbs. This time she couldn't trace the source. The koala had lost interest in her and the cockies were making a big deal of grooming their already pristine white plumage. There was a gardener on the far side of the barbecue area but he was fixing a mower and had his back to her.

Obviously she was imagining things. Again.

Paula snored on, mouth open. If anything or anyone pounced on Laura she could expect no help from that quarter.

She stood up and stretched. It seemed a shame to waste the day watching Paula catch flies. Tariq and her other friends were not due for at least an hour. What harm would it do to take a stroll? The reserve was quiet but not lonely. There were gardeners working and she'd seen a smiling family of campers and a couple of elderly walkers go by. If she ran into trouble, there were plenty of people to call on.

Being on her own in nature calmed her. The shrubs

and pale-trunked gum trees twitched and shimmered with happy birds. Laura had taken the liberty (another!) of borrowing Paula's pocket bird book. By the time she reached the lake she'd seen brilliantly coloured lorikeets and a superb fairy-wren with a bobbing metallic blue tail. Kookaburras laughed in the trees, but it was the cheeky grey galahs with their fluffy rose-pink chests that stole her heart.

The walk allowed Laura to put the bathroom incident into perspective. Sitting by the water, she tried sorting fact from fiction.

BITS SHE WAS SURE OF

1. Nobody had been hiding in the bathroom. The shower curtains were tied back and there were no storage cupboards.
2. The door was shut when she fainted but open when Mrs Brooksby found her.
3. The broken tap stopped spouting without being touched, meaning that the water was shut off remotely. Pinning down whoever was responsible for that was tricky. A team of 'tradies' – Aussi tradesmen – had been on school premises with access to the mains in the basement since eight a.m. The kitchen staff arrived even earlier. The basement was off-limits to pupils but almost any adult could have accessed it.
4. According to Tariq, Laura was not the only one late for the coach. A group of boys had gone MIA

after discovering an army-style obstacle course and Izzy was found sobbing in a linen cupboard because she was homesick. In the meanwhile, Paula and Tariq got off the bus to find Laura. As a result, it was impossible to say definitively who was where when.

BITS SHE WAS UNSURE OF

1. Whether she'd been locked in on purpose. The door had a quirky handle and she'd been dizzy. Her hands had been slippery too. It was possible that it hadn't been locked at all.
2. Why she'd fainted. Was it jetlag or did the chemical smell have something to do with it? The tradies had been spraying the fruit trees for pests and had also unblocked a drain. Could something toxic have drifted through the vents?
3. Whether or not she'd really seen a Joker in the steam. Whoever sketched it was no artist. Could they have been attempting something different?

SUSPECTS

1. The Straight As? A theory so far-fetched it was practically on the moon. Ed Lucas and The Cipher aside, all known gang members were in jail.
2. A prankster? If so, was it a classmate or grown-up? Was anyone she knew good at conjuring tricks? Had she upset anyone without realising it?

A third scenario popped into Laura's head. Was it possible that the intended victim was someone else?

Before she could ponder the matter further, a scream cut through the quiet. Laura leapt to her feet, heart hammering. The terrifying cry had come from the direction of the picnic area. Either Paula had woken up to find her gone and panicked, or something terrible had happened.

Even at an Olympic sprint, the picnic spot was further than she remembered. A fierce stitch was biting into her side when she rounded a gum tree and smacked hard into someone running the other way.

The man came off worse. Laura's shoulder rammed him in the spleen. He bent double, wheezing.

She took a cautious step towards him. 'Gosh, I'm so sorry. I – are you injured?'

The sight of her had the most extraordinary effect on him. He reeled away from her, croaking something unintelligible.

It was then that Laura was struck by what Matt Walker would have called a 'wrong note'. Though she'd only seen the gardener fixing the mower from a distance, she was sure he was the same man. He had a distinctive ring of clipped grey hair around an otherwise bald head. Yet this gardener's hands were free of dirt, oil and callouses. His fingernails were spotless.

A chilling possibility came to her. What if *he* was the cause of the scream? He looked ordinary enough but that meant nothing. Why else would he race away from a girl in distress, not towards her?

She edged sideways. 'Sorry again, but I need to get back. My friends will be wondering where I am.'

With startling speed, he straightened and advanced on her, blocking the path. 'Wait.'

Laura had no intention of waiting for anything. 'STRANGER DANGER!' she screamed, attempting to dart around him.

He grabbed her arm. 'No, you've got it all wrong. If you'd only—'

'STRANGER DANGER!'

There was a shouted response. The crack and crash of vegetation indicated the rapid approach of a rescue party. Laura took advantage of the diversion to spring out of range. When she looked back, the gardener had melted into the brush.

Jason Blythe reached her first, followed by Tariq and Roscoe. 'Laura, what are you doing here? Did you see the gardener? Did he harm you?'

'No, but—'

'Which way did he go?'

'I'm coming with you, Mr Blythe,' declared Roscoe. 'I'll be back-up,' he added boldly.

Jason's protests were cut short by the sound of a boat engine starting. They sprinted away towards the lake.

Tariq was looking at her strangely. 'We'd better get back before Mr Gillbert loses his mind. I don't think he could cope with three disasters in one day.'

She ran to catch up with him. 'What three disasters? Tariq, what's wrong?'

He stopped. 'A lot of people have been worried about

you this morning, me included. For all anyone knows, you could have concussion. Just for once, you could have done what you were told. You could have taken it easy. But, no, you can't stand rules, even if they're for your own good. Here you are, waltzing around on your own in the woods in the baking heat, asking for trouble.'

Laura stared at him in disbelief. 'I – umm.'

'Don't worry. Me and Elspeth covered for you. When we got here, Paula was asleep. When she woke up, she had a fit because you were missing. I said I was pretty sure I'd seen you heading off to the bathroom. Elspeth offered to check. That's when the gardener pounced on her.'

'The psycho?'

'He's not a psycho,' Tariq said crossly. 'He might have saved Elspeth's life.'

'Why was she screaming?'

'She didn't realise he was helping till afterwards. He leapt out of the bushes and prevented her from walking into a redback spider nest. That's not the only drama we've had today. Elspeth's been a bit of a legend.'

'You've only been gone for a few hours!'

'You'd be surprised what can happen in a few hours.'

Laura inhaled. 'Maybe you should start from the beginning.'

'After we left St George's we drove to Daylesford and then on to this place called Foster's Lookout. From there, it's a short hike to Simmons Reef. It's so cool. You can see the old sluices, tunnels and open-cut mines. I wish you'd been with us, Laura. The place was so thick with atmosphere you could almost taste it.

'Jason – Mr Blythe, I mean – loves telling stories. He told us that about ten years after the gold rush started these two men from Cornwall found a sixty-nine-kilogram nugget at the base of a tree in Bulldog Alley right here in Victoria. It's still the biggest ever found. In today's money it would be worth about three and a half million pounds.'

'We'd better walk and talk,' said Laura. 'What happened next?'

'We found a shady lunch spot. It was boiling and we'd walked a long way so after we'd eaten, the teachers decided we should rest. I fell asleep and so did lots of other people, including Mr Gillbert. Nobody noticed that Merryn and Naomie were missing until we were getting back on to the coach.'

Laura couldn't believe that while she'd been sitting reading half-baked conspiracy theories, a real drama was raging nearby. If only she'd been there. She could have helped.

'Mr Gillbert wanted to call the emergency services but Jason argued with him. He said we shouldn't waste police time until we'd done a proper search. They nearly came to blows.

'That's when Elspeth cut in, cool as can be. She'd seen Merryn and Naomie whispering and giggling on Dead Man's Hill. She said that maybe they'd decided to prank everyone by disappearing like the girls in *Picnic at Hanging*

Rock. She remembered Merryn reading it before we even came to Australia.'

Laura felt a stab of envy. If she had been there, would she have been the detective in the situation rather than Elspeth? But, no, of course she wouldn't because she'd only learned the story by reading *When Kings Go Missing.*

'Mr Gillbert wanted to send out a search party, but Jason suggested getting the bus driver to start the engine first. His theory was that if the girls were hiding nearby, they'd come racing out if they thought they were going to be left behind.'

Laura was surprised. Maybe the PE teacher was brighter than he looked. 'Inspired.'

'It was a bit,' agreed Tariq. 'And he was proved right. The girls were only hiding behind a clump of shrubs. They were in tears because they'd thought the coach was about to go without them. Until then, I don't think they'd thought through the consequences of playing hide and seek in the wilderness.'

He and Laura had reached the picnic area. Elspeth hurried up to them.

'Laura, I have to talk to you. Did you hear – a knight in gardeners' overalls snatched me away from a redback spider? But that wasn't the weird part.'

'No?' Laura looked past her to the hummingbird cake on the picnic table. There were four pieces left. 'Would you mind if we get some cake while you tell me about it? It's stuffed with pineapple, banana and pecans. Apparently, it's yum. We should get some before the cockies beat us to it.'

Elspeth stood her ground. 'Laura, I think he mistook me for you – the gardener, I mean.'

She had Laura's full attention now.

'That's impossible. I don't know anybody in Australia and you and I don't even slightly resemble one other.'

Tariq looked from Laura to Elspeth. 'I've never noticed it but, aside from the glasses, you sort of do. Elspeth's hair is longer than yours but it's the same colour and you have similar noses. You're also about the same height and—'

'We both have long, skinny legs,' Elspeth put in.

'We are not remotely alike,' insisted Laura. 'Even if we were, what made you think he knew me?'

'Because just before I walked into the spider's nest, he shouted, "Laura, no!" I got such a fright I screamed the place down. After I realised he was only trying to help, I said, "I'm not Laura Marlin, I'm Elspeth." Well, you should have seen his face. He took off running and next thing we heard you yelling.'

Paula came rushing over. 'Laura, I'm so sorry. The heat – I must have fallen asleep. I feel terrible. When I saw you were gone, I was worried you'd fainted again. Where were you?'

Laura lifted her hands vaguely. Before anyone could press her further, Jason Blythe and his young deputy strode from the forest.

'Mr Blythe, how did you get on?' Paula wanted to know. 'Any sign of the gardener? He's definitely not a reserve employee. I've spoken to the manager.'

Jason wiped his red face with the back of his hand. 'We gave it our best shot but he got away. I mainly wanted to thank him for helping Elspeth but I also wanted to ask him a couple of questions. If he was innocent, why would he run like that? We saw a boat speeding across the lake but it was too far to tell who was driving. Now, Roscoe, I don't know about you but after all our efforts I'm ready to eat a horse and chase the rider. How about some cake?'

Paula and Tariq went with them.

Elspeth turned to Laura. 'Let's say the gardener did mistake me for you. Was he a friend or a foe?'

'What's happening?' asked Camilla, swanning up. 'What are you talking about?'

Laura scowled. 'Elspeth has got it into her head that we look alike. Which we do not.'

'Do,' said Camilla with finality.

11

IF IT HADN'T been for the mix-up by the airline it might have been days before Laura heard the news. Instead she found herself sitting beside Mr Gillbert in Business Class.

'You don't have to look so glum about it,' said her teacher as he strapped himself into his seat and tested out the extra legroom. 'Most people would be thrilled to be upgraded. I certainly am. Or is it because you're next to me? I don't bite, you know – unlike almost everything in Australia.'

'I'll swap places with you, Laura,' volunteered Nicco, overhearing on his way to the back of the plane, where Tariq and the others were sitting with Paula and Jason

Blythe. 'I'd much rather have the posh food you'll get than the miniature dogs' dinner they'll serve us in cattle class.'

'Nobody is swapping with anyone,' snapped Mr Gillbert. 'Passengers are assigned seats for good reason. You'd do well to remember that millions go hungry every day, Nicco. Many would dearly love the economy class meal for which you're so ungrateful. As for you, Laura, you've been with your friends twenty-four/seven since we left the UK. Surely you can survive without them for the four and a half hours it takes to get to Darwin.'

Ordinarily Laura wouldn't have minded, but she'd finished her book and didn't fancy trying to make small talk with deathly dull Mr Gillbert. No doubt he'd make her employ the time usefully by writing in her Australian travel journal.

'Newspaper, sir?' The flight attendant was beaming down at Mr Gillbert. She fanned out a selection. 'I have the *Herald Sun,* the *Daily Telegraph,* the *Wall Street Jour*—'

'All of them!' cried Laura. The grown-ups stared at her in astonishment. 'Please.'

'I had no idea you were so interested in current affairs, Laura,' commented Mr Gillbert as the papers piled up on Laura's lap.

His pupil didn't hear him. She was staring aghast at the photo on the front page of the *Telegraph*. A smiling Ed Lucas was relaxing in a deckchair on a sun-drenched beach. He held a dewy cocktail in one hand and a postcard in the other. The message on it had provided the paper with its headline.

WISH YOU WERE HERE!

EX-DEPUTY PM MOCKS POLICE FROM BRAZIL AS STRAIGHT As SNATCH GREAT GATSBY IN PARIS

Bungling British detectives have been left with egg on their faces as one of the world's most wanted men taunted them from a beach in South America.

Forty-eight hours after staging a prison escape worthy of a Bond film, Ed Lucas, the alleged leader of the Straight A gang, appears to be beyond the reach of the law in a Brazilian paradise.

Expert analysis has confirmed that the photo is genuine. The Brazilian newspaper on the table beside Mr A has Saturday's date on it. Scotland Yard detectives are flying to Rio de Janeiro to make enquiries, but a source close to the investigation fears it's already too late.

'Given their failure to recapture the many hundreds of dim-witted burglars who abscond from Britain's open prisons every year, I'd say that the chances of Scotland Yard hunting down a man of Mr A's intellect and cunning in the Amazon jungle are slim to none. I'm hoping for the best but expecting the worst, put it that way.'

In a further blow for the authorities, a gang claiming to be the Straight As broke into iconic Paris bookshop, Shakespeare & Co., in the early hours of Saturday morning. The gang got away with the world's most valuable rare book: a first edition of F Scott Fitzgerald's *The Great Gatsby*, worth over £250,000.

For Love of Honey, a Victorian beekeeping manual by TR Llewellyn, worth just £50, was also missing.

The Straight As were believed to have been destroyed by

a series of high-profile arrests. Following the robbery, the notorious gang proved they're very much alive by leaving a Joker on the doorstep of Shakespeare & Co.

As the plane powered into the air, Mr Gillbert reached over and tapped the *Telegraph* article with his pen. 'Bit of a comedown in the world for Mr A and his boys, hey? Ed Lucas has gone from living the high life as a billionaire criminal in Her Majesty's Government . . .'

He paused and scratched his chin. 'Isn't it interesting how often they're the same thing? Now Lucas is a beach bum in Brazil and the sorry remnants of his gang have taken to stealing from bookshops rather than banks. A sure way to go broke. Although I will say this for the Straight As, they have good taste in literature.'

Laura looked at him. 'You're a fan of *The Great Gatsby*?'

'What? No, I prefer Hemingway myself. I was referring to TR Llewellyn's great work. Modern beekeepers are always on the lookout for quick fixes. An Australian father and son caused much excitement in the world of apiculture a couple of years ago by inventing something called a Flow Hive. Has a tap on the side. A tap! No more messing about with sticky trays or dressing up in a biohazard-type suit. A toddler can fill a jar with honey.'

Laura was puzzled. 'Isn't that a good thing?'

'It's a tragedy is what it is,' cried Mr Gillbert. 'The artistry, the *Zen* of beekeeping as defined by the great physicist TR Llewellyn, has been abolished at a stroke.'

Victorian beekeeping would normally have ranked alongside cement manufacturing on Laura's top ten list of subjects she didn't need to hear about before she died. But after Elspeth's *Great Expectations* and *Picnic at Hanging Rock* triumphs, she was open to tackling every obscure topic that came her way.

Besides, honey could be useful to a detective. In *Sting in the Tale*, Matt Walker had trapped a murderer by proving he'd been in the Scottish Highlands rather than Bognor Regis, as he claimed, because the raw heather honey the victim had been eating before she died came from the same stretch of moorland as the jar in his kitchen cupboard.

She gave Mr Gillbert her best smile. 'Sherlock Holmes was a beekeeper. After he retired from 221b Baker Street, he moved to the Sussex Downs and became an ape . . . uh, apiarist. In *His Last Bow* he tells Dr Watson that he watches the little working gangs of bees as he once watched the criminal world of London.'

Mr Gillbert glowed as if he'd swallowed a string of Christmas lights.

'You're so right, Laura! Historically, there have been many famous apiarists and indeed Holmes was one. Aristotle, the Ancient Greek philosopher and scientist, was known as the first "scientific beekeeper". I would argue that all he did was create myths about bees that took centuries to correct, but what do I know. Oh, and Hippocrates, the Father of Medicine, used honey as a cure for everything from ulcers to digestive complaints. Nowadays, manuka honey is used for burns and wounds.'

The trolley rattled to a stop beside him. 'Would you like champagne with your breakfast, sir?'

Mr Gillbert enthusiastically agreed to a Buck's Fizz

and a full breakfast, which was served with a tablecloth and proper china and as lovingly cooked as Nicco had imagined.

Laura said yes to an orange juice and a warm croissant spread with melting butter and strawberry jam. To the flight attendant's irritation, she asked for her cooked breakfast to be served to the boy in Economy seat 45A.

Mr Gillbert eyed her with new respect. 'That was kind of you, Laura. Now where were we? Famous beekeepers. Sir Edmund Hillary, who with Tenzing Norgay became the first mountaineer to summit Everest, thought of himself as a humble beekeeper till the day he died. But my own beekeeping hero is TR Llewellyn, whose book was stolen from the Paris bookshop. He was a physicist – self-taught, would you believe. His thoughts on the mathematics of the hexagon pre-dated the solving of the Honeycomb Conjecture by the University of Michigan's Thomas Hales by more than a century.'

Already sleep-deprived, Laura battled to stay conscious as Mr Gillbert droned on about the geometry of wax walls. She drifted off as he was listing the unending challenges facing bees.

When she came to, three minutes or perhaps three hours later, Mr Gillbert was talking animatedly about uranium hexafluoride. '"Hex", they call it.'

Laura decided that her capacity for learning about all things bee had reached its upper limit.

'Sorry to interrupt, Mr Gillbert. I urgently need the bathroom . . .'

Ducking under the curtain that separated Business from Economy, she sought refuge in the back of the plane. Camilla glowered at her as she went by. She was convinced that Laura had been singled out for special treatment. Nothing would persuade her that a computer error was responsible.

Nicco dragged himself away from the kickboxing film he was watching long enough to give her two thumbs up. 'Cheers, Laura. Breakfast was delish. The others were well jealous. I owe you one.'

She laughed. 'You're welcome.'

Tariq appeared to be asleep and she was reluctant to disturb him. Paula and Jason Blythe were in deep discussion. As she passed, their eyes slid sideways and they gave her the same fake smile. Laura's suspicions were instantly aroused. What or who were they discussing?

The emergency door next to the galley at the back of the plane had a large window. She peered out.

'Seen anything interesting?'

Laura immediately felt better. Best friends tend to have that effect, even – and perhaps especially – if you've recently disagreed. 'Only the world's biggest cloud duvet,' she told Tariq. 'Wouldn't it be cool if we could bounce on it?'

She took the *Telegraph* article from her pocket and handed it to him. 'By the way, you were right all along. The Straight As have got bigger fish to fry than two annoying kids from Cornwall.'

He read it quickly. 'Does this mean we can forget about them now? Maybe forever?'

'We can try,' Laura said, but the tightness in her stomach belied her words.

'Why so serious?' A flight attendant called Rebekah was smiling down at them. 'You're far too young to have any worries. Check out the view you're missing.'

The cloud had dissolved. The shadow of the plane was tracking across the Simpson Desert. From the air, it looked inviting. Laura pictured herself in a Lawrence of Arabia headdress, riding a camel over its raspberry ripple dunes. At school they'd learned about Robyn Davidson, a young woman who'd walked 1,700 miles across Western Australia with two camels and a dog.

Rebekah leaned between them. 'Hard to believe that anything but scorpions could survive out there, isn't it? But one of the world's last uncontacted tribes lived in the Gibson Desert until the eighties, when they reached out to relatives. They're known as the Pintupi Nine. Indigenous Australians are the most ancient civilisation on earth, you know. They've been around for over fifty thousand years.'

As they watched, the desert gave way to twisting deep blue creeks, curly-topped gum trees and specks of cattle.

'It's like an Albert Namatjira painting,' Tariq said. 'We saw some in a gallery in Melbourne yesterday. Maybe you've heard of him. He's a legendary . . .'

'. . . Aboriginal artist.' Rebekah laughed. 'I'm a fan. For me, he captures the spirit of what Indigenous Australians call "country". That's not the same as saying "the countryside", in case you're wondering.'

Laura glanced up. 'How is it different?'

Rebekah's brow wrinkled. 'Know what DNA is?'

'Of course! It's the unique genetic fingerprint of every living thing.'

'Then you'll appreciate that in Aboriginal culture there's no separation between them and the natural world. What it's taken the rest of us a couple of thousand years to learn, that we share our DNA with the trees, kookaburras and koalas, they've known all along. So, you see, tribes such as the Pintupi or Jawoyn don't just live in the country. They *are* country.'

She smiled. 'I'd better go. The duty free trolley is calling.'

Tariq was wistful. 'Wish I had a parachute. I'd float down there right now.'

'Dangerous things, parachutes,' commented Jason Blythe. 'They have a habit of not opening.'

He was propped against the galley wall as if he'd been there for a while. Laura wondered how much he'd overheard.

He flashed his boyish smile. 'Luckily, we'll be landing soon. You won't have to risk your neck, Tariq. Hope you're prepared for Australia's Wild West. Rumour has it that wherever you go in the Top End, you're never more than spitting distance from a snake, a croc or an outlaw.'

'And sometimes all three!' joked Laura, testing him. She had a sudden urge to see what, if anything, lay behind Mr Blythe's goofy grin.

The plane gave a violent lurch. The intercom chimed. Passengers were ordered to sit down and fasten their belts.

Jason whooped as if he were on a rollercoaster at

Disney World. 'You heard the captain, kids. Unexpected turbulence ahead. Better hurry back to your seats and buckle up tight. You're in for a bumpy ride.'

12

'IT'S NOT FAIR,' moaned Zach as the coach chugged along the coast road out of Darwin. 'Why can't I go in the Cage of Death? That's all I've thought about for weeks. Me and a saltwater croc eye to eye. I'd stare that sucker down. I wouldn't even blink.'

Giles Gillbert stifled a groan. It had been a relief to have an intelligent conversation on the plane with Laura Marlin, an odd girl but one who'd warmed his heart with a hitherto unsuspected interest in bees.

Mostly, he found today's children an enigma. He often thought he'd been born in the wrong century. In Victorian times, he could have whiled away the hours discussing royal jelly with refined, brilliant men such as TR Llewellyn. Instead he was a Year 6 teacher in the twenty-first century, where he was trying, and failing, to keep up with Snapchat, vloggers and the white cliffs of paperwork generated by the lunatic policies of successive government ministers.

And now he had the responsibility of keeping twenty-eight children alive for nearly a week on Australia's wildest frontier. Mr Gillbert thought gloomily of the lawsuits that would ruin him if even one of these little darlings keeled over with sunstroke or was stung by, say, a bull ant.

Across the aisle of the coach, Elspeth Roper had her nose in *Croc Attack*. Mr Gillbert prided himself in nurturing a love of reading in his pupils, but Elspeth's taste in literature was eccentric. If it were up to him, her entire holiday reading list would have been left behind in England. Unfortunately, the books had been bought for her by her mother, a woman who'd gained notoriety after arriving at the school gates in a pink convertible and matching stetson. As such he could do nothing to stop Elspeth poring over gruesome, true-life tales of the hapless humans who'd ended up on the menu of saltwater crocs.

'Salties,' he'd learned, were the dangerous ones. 'Freshies' were small, shy and lived mainly on birds, fish and rodents. They couldn't swallow anything larger than one's fist. Personally, Mr Gillbert found that to be of no comfort whatsoever.

Jason had tried to reassure him by comparing freshwater crocodiles to Chihuahuas. 'Salties are the Rottweilers of the creeks. They're the bities you really need to fret about.'

Like all Australians, Blythe had a habit of giving the

many menacing creatures in his country cutesy nicknames in an attempt to make them appear charming rather than deadly.

'*Please*, Mr Gillbert,' whined Zach. 'Surely we could squeeze Crocosaurus Cove into our schedule? It would make my year if I could go in the Cage of Death.'

Mine too, Mr Gillbert was tempted to reply but restrained himself.

Lee leaned over the back of his seat. 'What's the Cage of Death? Sounds excellent.'

'It's like a shark-diving cage, only made of glass. They lower you into an aquarium packed with crocs and dangle some meat over them. If there's a feeding frenzy you're right in the middle of it. It's soooo great.'

'Not for the crocodiles it isn't,' said Tariq. 'They'd rather be living peacefully in a quiet creek.'

Elspeth glanced up from her book. 'Tariq's right. Those close encounter experiences are always going wrong, Zach. One time a cable snapped on the Cage of Death and two people were plunged to the bottom of the croc pool. They were rescued in two minutes and were supposedly never in danger, but then that's what these places always say.'

'Killjoy,' muttered Zach.

'Where does she get this stuff?' Camilla asked Aaliya, not bothering to lower her voice.

Elspeth smiled. 'Just stating facts. Did you see the video of that massive shark smashing into a cage in Mexico—'

'That's quite enough, Elspeth!' Mr Gillbert broke in. 'Zach, the entire point of travelling fifteen thousand kilometres to Australia is so we can enjoy meeting crocodiles in their natural habitat. Otherwise we could have saved a fortune by visiting London Zoo. But don't worry. You'll see all the crocs your heart could desire in the Katherine Gorge.'

'Saltwater ones?'

'Absolutely.'

This was a lie. He had, in fact, done his best to get a guarantee from a Nitmiluk Park ranger that the section of the Katherine Gorge in which the St Ives party would be camping was saltie-free. In particular, he wanted clarification on the fluorescent green monster that had nearly cost the tourist his hand.

'Has *that* croc been eliminated?' he'd asked on a long-distance call. 'The one that was on the news and in all the papers.'

The ranger thought it the funniest question he'd heard in years. 'Yeah, and while we were at it we got rid of the infrared piranhas and levitating wallabies in Supernatural Creek,' he spluttered.

'Excuse me?' said Mr Gillbert. 'There's a lot of static on the line and I'm battling to hear. What was the name of creek?'

But the ranger was laughing too hard to reply.

Only after Mr Gillbert sternly reminded him that the lives of twenty-eight children and three teachers were at stake did he seem able to grasp that this was no joking matter.

'Mate, I give you my word there are no glowing green salties in the gorge. You know what these reporters are like: if a budgie burped, they'd say a cassowary caused a hurricane . . . What's a cassowary, you say? It's a large, flightless bird from the same family as emus and ostriches. Generally timid but if it gets alarmed it'll disembowel you, no problem. We don't have any in the park so you can cross that off your worry list.'

As Mr Gillbert made a mental note to add 'random cassowary attacks' to the twelve-page school disclaimer form, the ranger took pity on him.

'Look, there are no guarantees where Mother Nature is concerned, but our croc management team is first class. If the gorge floods, we get the odd saltie swimming downriver, but that's not likely to happen until January or so – long after you've gone. Trust me, my friend, you and your littlies are going to have the time of your lives.'

Recalling the conversation, Mr Gillbert prayed that his pupils would have the time of their lives for all the right reasons. But somehow whenever he thought about the upcoming gorge adventure a queasy knot formed in his stomach.

The coach slowed and turned into the crowded car park at Mindil Beach. Relief washed over Mr Gillbert. The Sunset Market would provide a much-needed distraction from his thoughts.

'Remember to stick together,' he cautioned as his charges leapt off the coach with ecstatic squeals.

It was hopeless. Mr Blythe was already leading a band of boys on to the beach to play Frisbee. Paula, the teaching assistant, who to Mr Gillbert's mind was doing precious little assisting, had formed a conga line with a group of girls. They danced through the palm trees on to the creamy sand.

Mr Gillbert followed dolefully, massaging his left temple to fend off a headache. It was after six p.m. but heat radiated up from the ground as if the earth's molten core was on the verge of erupting.

Six more days. All he had to do was keep the children out of harm's way for six measly, peasly days, one of which was almost over.

How hard could it be?

13

LAURA WAS TOO hot to join the conga line. She hung back with Izzy and Mia, feeling as if she were a cartoon dragon about to breathe fire. Though it was past six p.m., her arms were shimmery with sweat. Elspeth, trailing behind, had actually removed her cardigan. Only Tariq was in his element. His white T-shirt was as box-fresh as it had been when they left Melbourne early that morning.

'Bengali genes,' he told Laura with an apologetic grin. 'In the quarry where I worked, forty degrees was common. This is a regular day for me.' Then he ran off to play frisbee.

The girls passed beneath the palm trees and came to a dazed halt. The sky was a riot of gold and pink. It rose-tinted the beach and gathering crowd. Paula unfurled the picnic rugs with Laura's help. Mia and Izzy took selfies.

'Show's over, kids,' said Jason Blythe as the last ember of sun melted into the ocean, plunging the beach into darkness. He switched on a torch and began shepherding everyone towards the market. Beyond the dunes and palms, the lights of the stalls twinkled. 'Wait till you see the tucker on offer. Anything you fancy – candyfloss, hot dogs, Greek food, Thai, Vietnamese or vegan, it's all there. You have your vouchers. You can eat your heart out.'

At the market entrance, he raised his voice above the din: 'Now I don't want to sound like Giles Gillbert, but please stick together.'

Ignoring Mr Gillbert's glare, he went on: 'Naomie and Merryn, are you listening? I don't want anyone else going missing on my watch. We'll be looking out for you but you can assist us by keeping your friends close. Anyone caught going walkabout on purpose – Laura Marlin, I'm looking at you – will be about as popular as a rattlesnake in a lucky dip.'

Mindil Beach Market was an electric and eclectic mix of crafts, music and the aromatic delicacies of East and West. A local band led by a tangle-haired Aboriginal youth added to the carnival atmosphere. Laura was hypnotised by the way he kept up a continuous tribal pulse on his didgeridoo, never taking his lips from it.

'When do you think he comes up for air?' she asked Tariq.

'Doesn't need to,' answered Jason Blythe. He was standing behind them, tanned arms folded across his chest. 'Truly gifted players use circular breathing. They blow out through the didgeridoo and breathe in through their nose more or less at the same time.'

His phone buzzed in his pocket. 'Excuse me, kids. Gotta get this . . . Hi honey, give me a mo. Let me find a quieter spot.'

'I have to say, his habit of eavesdropping could get a little annoying,' Laura remarked as they moved with their group between food stalls.

Tariq gave her a reproachful look. 'What have you got against him? For the past five days, he couldn't have been nicer to us. To *you*. When you needed help in the Blackwood Reserve, he was the first to come running.'

'I never said I didn't like him,' hedged Laura.

'You didn't have to. Well, it's your loss. The rest of us want to start a petition to get him a job teaching PE at St Ives Primary. We think he's great. Compared to Jason, Mr Gillbert is the most boring teacher in the universe.'

'No, he's not,' snapped Laura, surprising even herself. 'He's a deep thinker and knows a lot of fascinating stuff. There's more to life than frisbees, you know.'

'Is that your problem with Jason – you don't think he's smart?'

Laura gave her best friend a quizzical glance. It was unlike him to be so defensive. 'I don't have any problem with Jas— Mr Blythe. What does it matter anyway? After we leave Australia, we're never going to see him again.'

She smiled. 'Hey, what do you fancy for dinner? I'm torn between Greek and Malaysian.'

But Tariq hadn't finished. 'Sometimes I think you were born suspicious, Laura Marlin.'

Mr Gillbert raised a hand to get everyone's attention. 'We're splitting into two groups. Those of you who want to eat first and look at boomerangs and crocodile belts later, come with me. Everyone else can go with Paula. Mr Blythe will join you shortly. Stand still, please. Let me count you.'

'I'm going with Paula and Jason,' said Tariq.

Laura hesitated for a fraction of a second. 'I'm going with Mr Gillbert.'

14

LATER, LAURA WAS able to pinpoint the exact moment she fell in love with Australia. It was while she was sitting on the dunes between the dark, swishing sea and sparkly stalls, enjoying a spicy coconut laksa soup. When she lay back on the warm sand and gazed up at the stars, the drone of the didgeridoo vibrated pleasantly in her chest.

She told herself that she didn't mind at all that Tariq was making new friends. They weren't Siamese twins. They were a crime-fighting team.

Laura sat up. Or were they? With the Straight As in jail or holed up in the Amazon, she and Tariq might never again stumble across a real mystery to solve. Even if they did, they might disagree there was a mystery in the first place. Tariq wasn't convinced that Laura had seen a Joker on the bathroom mirror at St George's, and she could hardly blame him. Truthfully, she doubted it herself. Three days on she'd yet to find a culprit.

She worried she was losing her detective touch. That was bad enough but it wasn't her only worry. She was convinced that something had happened to Skye. Three times she'd questioned her uncle about the husky's wellbeing and each time he'd evaded giving an answer. Once he'd joked that Skye was sulking because she'd chosen kangaroos over him. Then this morning, she'd received another cryptic text.

Away on business for a few days. Will msg when I can.
Rowenna manning fort. Speak when u r back from
Katherine Gorge. CR X

What business? Was he joining the hunt for Ed Lucas? And why was there again no mention of Skye? Was he ill or worse, had he run away? He had on occasion managed to leap from a window or sneak past their housekeeper, Rowenna, and come to find her at school. What if he'd done it again, only to find that she wasn't there? He might have gone further. She was forever reading about Border collies journeying hundreds of kilometres to find owners who'd moved house or gone on holiday. What if Skye had done the same? Would her uncle admit it or would he move heaven and earth to find him first?

Mr Gillbert broke into her thoughts. 'Anyone interested

in seeing a fire performer? Apparently, he's a highlight of the beach market.'

A skinny boy with a shock of black hair leapt to his feet. 'I am! I am!'

His teacher raised an eyebrow. 'Gosh, Oscar, I wish you were this animated in class. Usually, I'm on the point of checking your pulse for signs of life . . . Ah, now I remember. You're a budding magician, aren't you?'

'Fire artist, sir. Anyone with a smartphone can learn card tricks off YouTube but it takes years to learn fire skills. For my last birthday, my mum hired someone to teach me how to eat fire. I blew out such a huge flame that I nearly incinerated her rose bushes.'

Mr Gillbert raised an eyebrow. 'Gosh, she must have been proud. For Christmas, you might want to ask for a vacuum-deposited aluminised suit. Now, follow me, everyone.'

The market was packed to bursting. Laura was buffeted like a gull in a storm as she tried to get through the crowds to the front of the line. 'Hey, Oscar,' she puffed, 'can I ask you a question?'

'Sure.'

'I've seen you do card tricks but I was wondering if you knew anything about conjuring.'

He gave her a shy smile. 'I can't make a rabbit vanish from a hat, if that's what you mean, but I can do this . . .'

He opened his palm, revealing Laura's watch.

She took it in disbelief. 'How did you . . . ? Never mind. I have a question. Is it possible to make a ghostly image appear on a steamy mirror? You know, as a joke to scare someone.'

The smile left Oscar's face. 'You want to frighten someone? I'm not helping you with that.'

A streak of flame lit the night. Oscar sped up. Laura trotted to keep up with him. 'Please, it's important. Of course, I don't want to frighten anyone, but I think someone might have tried to scare me. All I'm asking is, is it possible to make writing appear on a mirror as if it's been drawn by an unseen hand?'

'Dead easy. You simply draw on the mirror with your finger shortly before any steam comes in contact with it. Whatever you've written becomes visible as soon as the mist starts rising. I tried it once before our cleaner started work on the bathroom. She screamed the place down. She's not spoken to me since.'

A shower of sparks lit the night. 'Thanks,' called Laura as Oscar darted away.

Swept along by the crush of people, she found herself in the smoky front row of Mindil Beach's most popular attraction. The fire dancer's black-clad frame and the tools of his trade – diabiolos, juggling torches and hoops – merged with the shadows behind him so that the fire took on a life of its own.

Flames spliced the darkness in spirals, twirls and arcs. They danced with the dancer, wrapping him in golden sheets of fire. Just when Laura was sure he'd be incinerated he emerged from the inferno, juggling his torches nonchalantly.

Dazzled, she glanced away to rest her eyes. Tariq was

standing a little way to her right with Elspeth, Nicco and Jago. She waved but someone tapped him on the shoulder and he turned without seeing her.

Inexplicably hurt, she looked away quickly. That's when she noticed the fake gardener from Melbourne.

Fear shot through her. She was about to alert Mr Gillbert when she realised that it was another case of mistaken identity. The man she'd seen at Blackwood was of medium height and build with a bland, pleasant face and a greying ring of hair. This man was at least six foot and had dark hair and a goatee beard. His Hawaiian shirt was plastered with palm trees silhouetted against a garish sunset. Why she'd confused him with the gardener was hard to say. Same body language perhaps.

Hawaiian shirt man was frowning at the crowd behind the St Ives kids and Jason. Laura tried to see who was so interesting but the school party was on the move.

'Come on, kids,' said Jason. 'Time to get you back to the hotel. Apologies to those of you who never had a chance to browse the market. We miscalculated the time and the coach driver needs his sleep. You'll thank me tomorrow. We have a very early start.'

As Mr Gillbert shooed the children before him, a carnival dragon sashayed in front of Laura, separating her from the group. She took the opportunity to glance back. Hawaiian shirt man was nowhere to be seen. The dragon took its time and Laura was running to catch her friends when she almost tripped over an elderly woman in a wheelchair. The woman's companion, a serious young Chinese, tutted in annoyance.

'You should slow down and be careful,' he scolded. 'Not everyone is as fit as you.'

Laura's cheeks burned with embarrassment. 'I'm so sorry. This is the second time this week I've banged into someone. I'm not usually so clumsy.'

The woman waved a hand heavy with rings. She had long, frizzy silver hair and wore a voluminous, colourful kaftan. 'My dear, Kim fusses far too much. I'm more robust than he believes. Think nothing of it.'

She took Laura's hand. 'Is that an English accent I hear?' Her voice was soft, with a sandpaper rasp.

Laura fought the urge to tug away. She glanced anxiously after her friends. They'd been swallowed by the crowd. Nobody had noticed her stop. She knew they were heading for the coach, but the parking area was large and chaotic and she didn't fancy negotiating it alone.

'Uh, yes, I'm with a school group from Cornwall. Sorry again about falling over you. If you're sure you're all right I'd better go. Our bus is about to leave.'

'Cornwall! Now there's a county with a dark and romantic history. Smugglers, moonshiners, highwaymen. I'd love to hear more but I won't detain you. You're understandably eager to rejoin your friends. Kim, I don't think it's safe for the young lady to find the school group by herself. It's bedlam here. Would you mind escorting her?'

She released Laura's hand in order to fan herself with a brochure. Though it was nine p.m., the heat was intense. 'I'd do it myself, dear, but it's slow progress in the chair. If you're elderly as well as differently-abled in the modern world, you might as well be a ghost. You're invisible.'

Laura apologised yet again, this time on behalf of her generation.

'Don't mention it. Pleasure to meet you. Go with Kim, dear. He's a Wing Chun master so you've nothing to be afraid of. Kim, I'll wait for you between these tents where I won't get knocked about.'

The last thing Laura wanted was to be helped anywhere by the unsmiling Kim. The fact that he was a martial arts expert made her more nervous still. He was a walking deadly weapon. Just because he cared for an old lady didn't make him trustworthy. She kept hoping that one of the teachers would return to rescue her.

'Thanks, Kim and Mrs . . . ?'

'Padrino. Widowed.'

'You're very kind, Mrs Padrino, but really no need. My teachers and friends won't be far. I think I see a couple of them . . .'

That's when it happened: a whiff of Mr A's expensive cologne tingled in her nostrils. Laura stared around frantically. Who or what was it coming from? Terror twisted in her gut.

'Is something the matter?' asked Mrs Padrino.

'No, I, uh . . . It's nothing.'

So distracted was Laura that she barely noticed as Kim began steering her behind a stall. 'This way best. Quicker to get to your friends.'

Before she knew it, they were leaving the crowded centre of the market and walking behind the tents and vans, through the shifting shadows of the trees.

Laura was feeling more uncomfortable by the minute.

'I think I'll be all right from here on. I'd rather look for my friends on my own.'

Without seeming to touch her, Kim propelled her forward. 'Not safe. I must take you. Mrs Padrino wants this.'

Hawaiian shirt man popped out of the shadows. ''Scuse me, folks. Any idea where I might find the Crocs Rock stand? It's the one that sells croc and kangaroo belts and so on.'

Kim barely looked round. 'Sorry, mate, I don't. Try the market directory.'

Hawaiian shirt man refused to be deflected. He smiled down at Laura. 'You look like a smart young lady. Do you know which stall I mean? They were engraving a crocodile wallet for me.'

'I think I do,' lied Laura. 'Kim, would it be okay if we show him? It'll only take a minute.'

Kim had no choice but to follow as they moved back to the main market. Hawaiian shirt man bombarded him with annoying questions. As they approached the line of tents, Laura spotted a narrow gap between two stalls. In a trice she'd slipped between them. She thought she heard a shout but the cacophony of world music made it hard to be sure. In seconds, she'd joined the flow of people heading for the exit. She didn't see Tariq until he was standing in front of her.

He did not look happy. 'This is positively the last time I'm covering for you, Laura. Why do you keep disappearing? I came back for you without telling anyone. Mr Gillbert will have a fit if he thinks you've gone missing again.

98

They're about to start roll call on the bus. We'd better run.'

Laura stayed where she was.

When he turned and saw her face, he paused too. 'I'm sorry. I don't mean to sound cross. It's just . . .'

'Just what?'

'You seem to be going out of your way to look for trouble, that's all. Mr A is in Brazil. You have photographic proof. He and the Straight As are someone else's problem now.'

Conscious that Kim might spot her if she stayed where she was, Laura started towards the car park. 'Since when do you believe everything you read in the papers, Tariq?'

'Since never, but—'

'Then you realise that at least half the story could be inaccurate?'

He threw up his hands. 'There you go again – questioning everything, being suspicious. We're on holiday, Laura. I don't want to be a detective on this trip. I want to have fun and be . . . normal. You know, just an ordinary, regular boy.'

Normal?

The word pinged painfully around Laura's brain. Never in her life had she had the slightest yearning to be regular or ordinary. Quite the reverse.

'Is that too much to ask?'

In the flicker of car park lights, he looked oddly vulnerable. Laura's heart went out to him. Because of her, he'd been dragged into all manner of dangerous situations all around the world. He'd been there for her through thick and thin. Nobody deserved a break more than Tariq.

'No,' Laura said. 'It's not too much to ask. Most definitely not.'

The coach was parked beneath a palm tree. Their classmates were milling about on the pavement. Jago had had an allergic reaction to his sun cream, Izzy had lost her purse and Camilla's sunglasses were missing. In the general chaos no one had noticed Laura and Tariq's absence. They emerged from the shadows just as Paula came flying out of the coach to say that Izzy's purse had been found beneath her seat and Camilla's sunglasses were on Mia's teddy bear.

As Laura waited to board the bus, Mr A's cologne drifted past on the night wind. It was stronger this time, as if he or whoever wore it were within striking distance. She didn't look round. She didn't dare.

15

THE STUART HIGHWAY stretched arrow-straight to the horizon before dissolving into a shimmering blue mirage. Laura wished it were real so she could dive into it. The air-conditioning on the coach had broken down. But she at least had iced water. The eucalypt woodlands and mango farms they passed crackled under the merciless sun. A fire risk warning sign flashed by, its needle turned to red.

A hawk swooped down and snatched something from the tarmac. From the front seat of the bus, Laura had a vivid image of its black-tipped wings, wedge tail and cruel beak as it whirled out of range.

'Black kite,' the bus driver told her. 'Indigenous

Australians call them "firehawks" and the fires they start "*jarulan*". They're deeply unpopular with our firies . . .'

'Firemen?' guessed Laura.

'That's right! The firies loathe them because the kites know that if they pick up smouldering twigs and drop them on dry grassland, they can start their own fires whenever they're feeling peckish. They'll snack on snakes, ground birds and lizards as they run for their lives.'

Jago wrinkled his nose. 'Chargrilled goanna. Nice.'

Laura stared out at the unending landscape. Everything in Australia seemed magnified: the weird and wonderful creatures, the elements, the wide-open spaces. Even the haulage vehicles that went by were not simply single lorries but 'road-trains' four trailers long, transporting oil, cement or sheep. The weight of their loads was such that drivers had to apply the brakes eight hundred metres before any stop. When they overtook the coach, the gale of their passing shook the children to their core.

'If a fire starts, how hard is it to put it out?' Laura asked.

'Out here, the flames can leap as high as skyscrapers. Most times the only way the firies can tackle it is to spray red firefighting foam from the air.'

He grimaced at the cloudless sky. 'We're desperate for rain, but that can be a mixed blessing if it brings flash floods and lightning. Last summer Darwin had 1,634 lightning flashes in an hour. Trees were exploding.'

Elspeth leaned over the back of the seat. 'Trees?'

'Correct. See, when termites gnaw out the centre of an ironbark tree they create a funnel. If the tree is then struck by lightning, the whole trunk blasts out of the ground.'

There was an awed silence while the listening Year 6s digested this.

'Life here is so extreme,' said Laura, half to herself.

The bus driver grinned. 'That's why we love it. The lows make the highs so much sweeter. In the Top End, people tend to live every day as if it's their last.'

Laura thought of Ed Lucas. Was that how he was living in his Brazilian paradise – as if every day was his last? Was he lying in a hammock drinking pina coladas and reading *The Great Gatsby*? Or had the book been sold to fund his new life?

She found it curious that he'd ordered his men to steal the Victorian beekeeping manual too. Was he, like Sherlock Holmes, planning a new career as an apiarist?

A sign loomed: Litchfield National Park.

'Get your belongings together,' ordered Mr Gillbert. 'We'll be stopping for a cup of tea in Batchelor in five minutes. Jago, if you don't want to get chargrilled yourself, please apply sunblock!'

First stop was the Magnetic and Cathedral Termite Mounds, some rising nearly four metres high. The children admired them from the roped-off viewing area.

'It's like Stonehenge,' said Mia, 'only built by ants.'

Mr Blythe nodded. 'That's true of the Magnetic ones especially. See how they're all so perfectly positioned, as if a termite city planning department has put up tombstone towers? They're aligned north to south. Termites are thin-skinned, you see. They like their cities to stay at a constant thirty degrees Celsius.'

The heat was relentless. So were the flies. The wilting children were relieved when the coach pulled into the car park of Florence Falls. There, a double waterfall cascaded into a monsoon forest. One hundred and sixty steps took them down to a deliciously cold green swimming pond.

'What about salties?' Camilla asked with a shudder.

'There are none in this pool,' the driver assured her. 'You're quite safe. We'll be here for some time so you might as well relax. Haven't you heard that the NT in Northern Territory stands for Not Today, Not Tomorrow, Not Tuesday, Not Thursday? Territorians never do anything in a hurry.'

The heat was so oppressive that Laura found it incredible that anyone with a real job was able to function at all. She barely had the energy to climb into the pool, but she was glad she did. It was exhilarating swimming at the base of the foaming, roaring waterfall.

'This beats the best Jacuzzi in the fanciest spa anywhere in the world,' said Naomie as she and Laura edged behind a curtain of falling water. Through the spray, Laura saw a figure on the high boulders that framed the waterfall. He had the shape of Hawaiian shirt man and seemed to be looking her way. A chill of fear rippled through her. She ducked out to get a clearer view but whoever it was had gone.

Egged on by Jason, the bolder children took turns in leaping off a slippery rock beside the waterfall. They pretended not to hear Mr Gillbert's plaintive appeals from the bank.

Afterwards, Laura sat in the shade studying Paula's bird book. Rainbow-coloured lorikeets chattered in the trees higher up the slope, nipping at the nectar in the eucalyptus flowers. According to the book, they made good pets and learned to talk easily. Laura preferred to see them free with their friends in the wild.

Tariq and Kyle explored the fringes of the pool, searching for interesting flora and fauna. Laura nearly had a heart attack when they disturbed a water dragon. It waddled from the foliage and down to the pond's edge.

Tariq lay on his stomach and wriggled nearer to it. When the great lizard swung its prehistoric head, they were suddenly nose to nose. Kyle was beside himself with excitement. 'Tariq, where's your phone? Let me take a photo.'

Using phones to look at social media had been banned by Paula but, following a complaint from a parent, she now permitted those children without cameras to use their smartphones. Kyle snapped away with the fervour of a paparazzi photographer.

Jason Blythe came to see what the fuss was about. 'You should use that as your school yearbook portrait, Tariq,' he said smilingly. 'Lizard Dundee, they'll be calling you.'

But after the goanna had shuffled away, bored with the attention, Tariq found the photos were unusable. Kyle's finger had obscured the lens in three of them and the rest were blurred or shot into the sun.

Kyle was embarrassed. 'Sorry, Tariq. I should have got

Laura or Mr Blythe to take the picture. I've always been hopeless with cameras.'

Tariq hid his disappointment well but Laura felt for him. It had been a once in a lifetime shot. To her surprise, it was Jason Blythe who saved the day.

'I might be able to patch them up. Email them to me, Tariq. I'll see what I can do.'

He was as good as his word. That evening at the Banyan Tree campsite he took out his laptop, a black, clunky contraption so battered it was hard to believe it functioned, and tapped away at it. Looks proved deceptive. Within minutes, Tariq's phone pinged and a brilliantly coloured, pin-sharp image of boy and lizard came up. Tariq didn't stop smiling all evening.

It was this generous act that finally won Laura over. When the petition to have Jason Blythe appointed as PE teacher at St Ives Primary was finally drafted, she made up her mind that she would be the first to sign it.

16

KATHERINE GORGE, NORTHERN TERRITORY, AUSTRALIA

'GOOD GRIEF!' EXCLAIMED Paula. 'What was that hideous cry? Do you think the previous school party is being devoured by savage beasts?'

'Supernatural Creek strikes again!' said Zach excitedly. 'What do you think it is this time – another glowing green crocodile? Or maybe infrared piranhas?'

He'd have rushed down the hill to the river if Jason Blythe hadn't caught his arm. 'Mate, we've all had a laugh about this, but the joke's getting a bit tired. Weren't you listening when the ranger at the Nitmiluk Visitor's Centre explained to us that the whole thing's been created by a couple of attention seekers and a croc attack victim who'd gone troppo. That what we call it here when the heat cooks your brain.'

'Yeah, well, I don't believe it,' sulked Zach. 'No smoke without fire.'

'Oh, yes, there is,' said Mr Gillbert. 'You know reporters. Never let the truth stand in the way of a good story. For your information, the park ranger also told us that he was there when the supposed glowing green croc was trapped and dragged from the water. Surprise, surprise, it was completely normal. Covered in weeds but just as large and ugly as any other saltie in the Katherine Gorge.'

Jason gave the Year 6s a sly grin. 'Couldn't have put it better myself. So from now on, let's all refer to Supernatural Creek by its proper name, Five-Mile Creek. Right, we'd better get going before we miss the four p.m. boat for the Nabilil Dreaming Sunset Dinner Cruise. Wait! There it goes again. Someone's screaming blue murder.'

Camilla clutched Paula's arm. 'Please let me go to a hotel. I'm sure my mum will pay. How many times do I have to tell everyone I'm not the outdoors type?'

A passing hiker solved the mystery. 'Nothing to fear, ma'am,' he told Paula. 'It's the grey-headed flying foxes rowing over who gets the best spot on the branch.'

Only mildly reassured, they proceeded down the track to the river. Laura tried to imagine what sort of foxes climbed trees. If small children weren't being murdered, perhaps the foxes were murdering each other.

Round the next bend an unforgettable sight greeted them: a line of gum trees almost black with the folded forms of fruit bats. So numerous were they and so tightly clustered that the smallest shift in position set the entire colony screeching. Combined with birdsong and the trill of the cicadas which gave Nitmiluk its Jawoyn Aboriginal name – 'place of cicadas dreaming' – the noise was deafening.

As they looked on, a branch snapped beneath the weight of a dozen flying foxes. Outraged at being displaced, they wheeled around like vegetarian vampires. Oscar was ready to faint with horror. Camilla was convinced they'd get entangled in her auburn bob. But Tariq and Laura were entranced. The bats peered down at them with their foxy brown faces, wings clasped to their chests as if in prayer.

A horn blast sent the friends racing to the dock. As Laura stepped aboard, a swell tossed the flat-bottomed boat. She overbalanced and would have plunged into the river without the lightning reaction of the boatman's teenage son, Billy. He hauled her to safety with astonishing strength. When she thanked him, a grin flashed in his dark face.

'No drama.'

Viewed from the deck of the Visitors' Centre, the Katherine Gorge had been spectacular, but Laura liked it best at water level. As the sun set, the pink sandstone cliffs blazed burnt orange and the wide brown river rippled with gold.

Shy freshwater crocodiles sank beneath the reeds as they passed.

Later, they moored at a rock art site and Captain Nipper told them about Puwurr, also known as the Dreamtime or Dreaming. In Aboriginal tradition, the Dreamtime was the creation period, when the world was made.

'Spiritual beings such as Pula, creator of the gorge and waterfalls, put themselves into country,' Captain Nipper said. 'They laid down the rules for proper behaviour and named everything in stories and songs and said who belonged to the land. They gave country its language.'

Something stirred in Laura's soul as she listened. For centuries, the thirteen gorges had been walked, fished and swum by the Jawoyn people, the custodians of Nitmiluk. Every feather, scale and grain of sand was precious to them.

'If it's always belonged to the Jawoyn, why is it called the Katherine Gorge?' she asked Billy, the boatman's son. He explained the Jawoyn people had only won the rights to their own land in 1989, 127 years after Scottish explorer John McDougall Stuart named the Katherine River after his expedition sponsor's daughter. To reclaim it Jawoyn Aboriginals had to prove it was theirs by taking government officials to sacred sites, women's business sites, birthing sites and others.

Finally, a stamped, signed deed confirmed to the world what local tribes had known all along: Nitmiluk was woven into Jawoyn DNA.

Dinner was crocodile or sweetcorn bisque, barramundi and coconut crème brûlée, by candlelight. Laura and Tariq found themselves seated beside Margo and Jett, an elderly couple from Darwin. They were celebrating their thirtieth wedding anniversary.

'You're an adventurous lot, visiting the Northern Territory in our wet season,' commented Jett. 'There's a huge storm system heading this way in the next couple of days. Hope you're not camping.'

'We are but we'll be fine,' Tariq told him. 'In England, we're used to camping in the rain.'

Jett chuckled. 'Son, there's rain and there's rain. When Tropical Cyclone Les hit Katherine in 'ninety-eight, the river rose fourteen metres overnight. After the flood waters subsided, people were finding crocs in their swimming pools. There were a couple in the butcher's department at Woolworths too. Had themselves a feast. All I'm saying is when the rain comes, take cover.'

His wife smiled. 'Jett's a pilot – hence the nickname. He's really called Bob. Like all pilots, he's obsessed with the weather.'

Tariq sat forward. 'We heard about the Flying Doctors crash. What do you think caused it – lightning or something else?'

Laura raised her eyebrows, giving him a *Now Who's Being Suspicious?* look.

'Just curious,' he muttered under his breath.

'I suppose you're referring to the UFO stories the tabloids concocted,' Jett retorted. 'Utter nonsense. I've known Eden Jackson, the pilot, all her life. She's the best of the best. The plane was a nearly new Polatus EC-12. Normally, the Flying Doctors don't service the Top End, but Care Flight, which does, was stretched to capacity. So Eden got the call. Nothing about that night was normal. Nothing at all.'

'Can you tell us what happened?' asked Laura.

'There was a lot of storm activity in the area that evening but nothing they couldn't handle. Eden told me that as she approached the thirteenth gorge, a dazzling flare appeared in the sky. She was still trying to work out what it was when the onboard computer system crashed. Total avionics failure. Pilot's worst nightmare. A blind emergency landing in pitch darkness in a wilderness.'

Tariq was on the edge of his chair: 'So what did she do?'

'The only thing she could do. Activated the ELT – the Electronic Locator Transmitter. Then Eden got them down as best as she could using a standby artificial horizon, compass and speed tape. The plane was a write-off but everyone survived. The croc bite victim they'd been on their way to save was rescued by the crew that came to help them. He's on the mend too. A happy ending all round!'

'But no aliens?'

Jett laughed. 'No aliens.'

'What about the light in the sky?' Laura said. 'Did Eden ever discover what it was?'

'No, but I have a theory.'

His wife nudged him. 'Jett, we should let these

youngsters get back to their friends. We can't monopolise them for the whole evening.'

Laura smiled. 'You're much more interesting than our friends. Go on, Jett, tell us your theory.'

Jett was proud to be asked. 'It was when Eden saw the flash that the readings on her cockpit computers went haywire. She wondered if the two things were related.'

He paused while the waitress set down a coffee pot and bowl of sugar.

'It reminded me of what happened with that Japanese doomsday cult. You'll be too young to remember how they released sarin nerve gas into the Tokyo subway. Twelve people died.'

Laura was taken aback. 'A Japanese cult? You think they're behind the Flying Doctor crash?'

'Good heavens, no. I merely mention them because of a peculiar coincidence. In 1993, Australian seismologists keeping an eye out for earthquake activity picked up a disturbance in the Great Victoria Desert. Their readings indicated an eruption 170 times more powerful than any mining explosion in history. At the same time, truck drivers saw a brilliant flash in the night sky and a pilot reported that the instruments on his plane went berserk. No cause was ever found.

'Fast-forward two years. Aum Shinrikyo, the cult, attack the Tokyo subway. Only then did investigators learn that they'd been busy mining uranium in Western Australia. Turns out, they'd hired two nuclear scientists, made a mini atomic bomb and carried out a controlled explosion. That's what our seismologists picked up, an atomic blast!'

Margo poked him in the ribs. 'Jett, these lovely kids came to Australia to experience the peace and beauty of our great country. Now they'll be imagining that there are cult loonies behind every pandanus tree.'

'No we won't,' Tariq assured her. 'It's a fascinating story.'

'We've had a great evening,' agreed Laura.

'All I'm saying is that there are similarities between the events in Western Australia and the Flying Doc crash here,' Jett said gruffly, 'not least that Eden was flying over a uranium mine when she saw the flare of light.'

His wife pursed her lips. 'A disused mine that was shut down thirty years ago, around the time I made the mistake of marrying you . . . Laura and Tariq, did you say you're from St Ives Primary? Our favourite holiday ever was a summer in Mousehole . . .'

Zipping herself into her sleeping bag at the end of the evening, it struck Laura that she hadn't given a thought to Mr A and his Brotherhood of Monsters all day. It made a pleasant change.

Sleep overtook her and she dreamed of the Dreaming.

17

'IS THIS IT?' Lee picked up a stone and skimmed it across the calm beige surface of Five-Mile Creek. 'Doesn't look very Supernatural to me. Where are the infrared piranhas?'

'What did you expect?' asked Merryn. 'Dancing unicorns?'

'Dunno. Something more thrilling than this.'

Tariq was incredulous. 'You're surrounded by real-life nature. What could be better than that? Already this morning, Billy – he's the boatman's son – has shown me fairy martins, kingfishers, blue-faced honeyeaters and paperbark trees. The bark from those can be used to make a portable oven. The Jawoyn even have their own seasons – five major and five minor. December is called Kuran.'

In the shade of the campsite marquee, Camilla yawned. She was rubbing her arms with a rapidly shrinking ice cube. 'I'd care more if I wasn't being boiled alive.'

'Apparently, there's a storm heading our way tomorrow,' said Merryn. 'That should cool us off. Hard to believe it'll happen though. Not a cloud in the sky.'

'You'd better believe it,' Jason Blythe told her, coming over with a football under his arm. 'Up here, storms form right in front of your eyes.'

Lee grinned. 'Poltergeist storms. Something supernatural at least.'

'That's right. Hey, anyone want to join me for a kickabout? Laura, how about you?'

Lost in her own world, Laura stared blankly at him. 'I'm sorry, what?'

'Footie? Aussie Rules? Want to join us?'

'No thanks, Mr Blythe.'

'Are you crook? That's Australian for sick by the way.'

'I'm 110 per cent, thanks, but it's a bit hot to chase a ball. I'm saving my energy for the tour of Nitmiluk Park later on.'

'So am I,' said Lee. 'Thanks though.'

After he'd gone, taking Tariq and Kyle with him, Laura retreated behind the bird book she was holding up to hide her phone. Tariq had accused her of being paranoid and suspicious and she was working hard on not being that way, but some days it was impossible. Today was one of them.

After half a dozen texts in which their housekeeper had sidestepped all questions about Skye, Laura had asked Rowenna for a photo of him. An hour earlier, her phone had pinged. On her screen was a cute shot of the husky and wolfhound curled up in front of the Aga, looking angelic.

As promised, Lottie & ur gorgeous boy xxx

Far from being reassured, Laura was now certain that something was dreadfully wrong. Rowenna was hopeless with technology. She'd sent the photo without realising that it revealed the date it was taken – six weeks earlier!

Laura stared miserably at the screen. How was she expected to blindly trust in people when even good, kind Rowenna was capable of betrayal? Where was Skye? Was he pining so much he'd become ill, or was he halfway across the country, searching for her? What if he was run over, or dead?

Skye wasn't her only concern. How could she relax when the same canoeist had passed their camp at least four times, each time wearing a different baseball cap and T-shirt? At one stage he'd even sported red hair.

He was quite tubby and not in the least like the rather muscly Hawaiian shirt man from the market, yet instinct told her they were the same man or part of a team, perhaps sent by the Straight As.

Either that or she was going mad, which was entirely possible.

She wished she could talk to Tariq but something had changed between them. Outwardly, they were still best friends, but emotionally, they weren't. It was as if something invisible divided them. A pane of glass.

For the first time since she'd left the orphanage, Laura felt intensely, excruciatingly lonely.

Elspeth put down her book. 'Maybe they're radioactive?'

Merryn blew on her newly painted nails. 'What's radioactive?'

'The glowing fish and crocs. Look what happened after the Chernobyl nuclear disaster in the Soviet Union in the eighties, and the more recent one in Japan.'

'Here we go,' Camilla whispered to Merryn. 'Another conspiracy theory.'

Elspeth flushed. 'They're facts. Look them up.'

Lee was bemused. 'What does Chernobyl have to do with fish in Australia?'

'Because for years afterwards scientists kept finding these monstrous mutated plants and fungi. Glowing ones too.'

'Nope, still don't get the connection. In case you hadn't noticed because, you know, because you've hardly looked up from your book since we left London, we're in a wilderness. No nuclear power plants around here.'

Laura's heart went out to the girl. 'If you ever let Elspeth finish a sentence, Lee, she might be able to tell you why she thinks they're connected.'

Elspeth gave her a surprised but grateful glance. 'Yeah, Lee, how do you know that there's not some evil factory spewing out chemicals upriver?'

'What evil factory?' demanded Wayne the campsite manager, marching up to them. 'You're in three thousand square kilometres of protected wilderness and you're worrying about factories. None for hundreds of miles.'

A thought struck Laura. 'What about the uranium mine? The one near the thirteenth gorge.'

Wayne looked uncomfortable. 'Ah, Mine 13. It was shut before you were born but it's a sore subject.'

'Why?'

'Uranium mining is a dark chapter in our nation's history. Gamma radiation and radioactive dust has been linked to cancer and other unexplained illnesses in Indigenous communities. Hundreds of Aboriginal families were forced to leave their ancestral lands in Western Australia because they became environmental disaster zones. And here in the Top End we had the notorious Rum Jungle mine. Acid drainage from the mine killed all plants and animals along a ten-kilometre stretch of the Finnis River.'

Laura remembered Paula's comment on Australia's new settlers: *Sadly, they had very short memories.*

The teaching assistant chose that moment to duck under the tent flap and announce that lunch was ready. 'What's keeping everyone?'

'Wayne was telling us about the uranium mine close to the last gorge,' answered Laura.

Paula threw up her hands. 'Why would anyone want to dig up and pollute such a glorious place? Uranium's radioactive waste alone – tailings, they call it – has a half-life of 4.46 billion years. Even after it's supposedly been disposed of, that's how long it continues to wreak havoc with the environment and human health.'

Merryn was aghast. 'What can possibly make it worth poisoning rivers and animals and forcing Aboriginal families out of their homes?'

'Atomic weapons,' Paula told her. 'In the fifties and sixties, the UK and Australian Governments got together to mine uranium and build nuclear bombs.'

Laura was shocked. 'The British were involved?'

'Yes, but remember that the world was different then. We'd had the Second World War and the Russians were a threat. People were afraid of a Third World War.'

Elspeth said what everyone was thinking: 'They still are.'

'The GOOD NEWS,' interjected Wayne, 'is that the thirteenth gorge mine has been leased by a sprightly widow determined to clean it up. She's quite a character, Mrs Padrino.'

Laura couldn't believe her ears. 'Mrs Padrino?'

'That's right. She's elderly and in a wheelchair. Her carer is a martial arts master of some kind. Not that she needs him. She's a tough old bird. Still travels the world and seems quite capable of taking care of herself.'

He rubbed his belly. 'Enough about mining. Let's go get us a goanna burger. Just kidding, Izzy. We have beef or carrot and cashew.'

Laura trailed behind as the group moved towards the barbecue area. She'd lost her appetite. Over the past eight days there'd been a great many coincidences. Mrs Padrino was one too many.

~ 18 ~

LAURA COULDN'T SLEEP. It was sweltering in the tent and Izzy was snoring. Her mind flitted from the news of Mr A's escape to the gardener at Blackwood. It went from the Japanese doomsday cult to Supernatural Creek to the rare books stolen from Shakespeare & Co and Mrs Padrino.

The same thread ran through everything. She just couldn't see what it was.

BITS SHE WAS SURE OF

1. Mr A was on the run

2. Mine 13 and the Flying Doctor crash were somehow linked
3. A series of strange people had accosted her or followed her or her classmates since their arrival in Australia

BITS SHE WAS UNSURE OF

1. Where Mr A was on the run
2. Who or what had caused her to faint in the bathroom at St George's School
3. Whether the man in the Hawaiian shirt was a Straight A villain
4. Whether there was any truth in the stories about fluorescent crocs and wallabies walking on water

That afternoon, Laura had borrowed Merryl's phone, which had a local SIM card. Getting any signal, let alone one strong enough to do a Google search, was tricky, but her patience was rewarded when she stumbled across a 1958 quote from Robert Menzies, then Australian Prime Minister. Opening the Rum Jungle mine, he told the crowd that whatever one's opinion of atomic bombs, 'our security in the present tremulous condition of world safety depends upon the superiority of the Free World in terms of these dreadful instruments.'

The Rum Jungle had been closed for decades but the issues around uranium hadn't gone away. There were scores of recent articles on battles between mining giants and Indigenous communities.

'We have sun, we've got wind, we've got people,' said pastor Geoffrey Stokes of the Wongatha clan. 'Why should we pollute our country for money?'

But other clan leaders disagreed. They wanted a share of the billions to help rebuild communities shattered by previous uranium mines.

It goes on and on, Laura thought to herself, *round and round in a loop.*

In the sleeping bag beside her, Izzy grunted and snuffled like a contented piglet. Laura sat up. She had to get out before she suffocated.

Out in the balmy air she felt better. The sky was so thick with stars it was almost silver. A movement caught her eye. The Jawoyn boy, Billy, was on the shore of Supernatural Creek. He knew it was her before he turned around.

'Couldn't sleep?'

'Too hot,' she said. 'Do you live near here?'

'In a way. Dad's job comes with a house. People judge us because we took out the doors and windows, but we Jawoyn don't do well with walls.'

'Who needs walls in a place like this? If I lived here, I wouldn't want anything between me and nature. Well, maybe a little something between me and the snakes. And spiders. And salties.'

He laughed. 'Salties are misunderstood, you know. There's no harm in 'em. It's only that they get big enough to eat you.'

Laura smiled back. 'That's all right then. What are you doing out here? You look as if you're waiting for someone?'

'Not some*one*. Some*thing*.'

The hair rose on the back of Laura's neck. She had a sudden sense that Billy knew something about the supernatural events at Five-Mile Creek. If she waited with him, chances were that she would too.

The silence stretched out, broken only by the cicadas. They stood side by side, staring at the dark water. Finally, Billy spoke. 'Do you believe in magic, Laura?'

'Harry Potter wizard magic or rabbit in a hat magic?'

'Real-life magic.'

'If it's real, how can it be magic?'

'Wanna see?'

Every instinct told Laura to return to the sanctuary of her stuffy but safe tent, but curiosity consumed her.

'Yes, I would. Very much.'

Billy led her along the creek's edge, beneath the sandstone cliffs. The shadows were as dense as treacle and Laura stumbled and slipped on stray rocks and driftwood. With every step, she was braced for the hiss or crunch that would mean the end of the toes or legs she was so fond of.

'Don't you think we should fetch a torch?'

Billy glanced round. 'Why? Can't you see?'

'In the pitch dark? No, I can't. Only superhumans like you have infrared vision. Billy, if you don't mind I'm going to turn back. I'll be in detention for the rest of my life if Mr Gillbert finds I've gone walkabout . . .'

'It's here.'

She hesitated. 'What's here?'

'Laura, you're going to have to trust me. Take off your shoes and step into the creek and you'll see the magic.'

'Are you insane? I wouldn't dip a toenail in that creek if you paid me a million dollars. No, make that ten million.'

Laura's skin prickled with fear. The lights of the campsite seemed a long way off. If she screamed, would anyone hear her?

She was turning away when Billy said softly: 'Your friend, Tariq. He told me you're a detective.'

Laura spun round. 'Why would he tell you something like that?'

'Because I heard you questioning the camp manager about Mine 13. He said you're always like that. You never accept what's on the surface. He told me you always want answers on what lies beneath.'

'So what?' Laura said defensively. 'What's so bad about that?'

He held up both palms to show he hadn't meant offence. 'In our culture, the one who asks questions and stands up for justice, we have a name for them. We call them Featherfoot.'

'Featherfoot?'

'In the old times, these detectives wore emu feather slippers to hide their footprints. This is you, I think. You're a Featherfoot.'

'Half a Featherfoot,' Laura corrected him. 'I need Tariq in order to be a whole one. We're a team.'

'You're a good friend. Loyal too. But right now Tariq is

not here. If you want answers, you're the one who has to be brave.'

'I'm not going in the water, if that's what this is leading up to,' Laura protested. 'N.O. No.'

'Laura, I was born here. This river runs in my veins like blood. Upon my honour, there are no salties here. When the storm comes, very likely there will be. But not now. Don't be afraid. The water is shallow.'

Laura's instincts had let her down before but she put her faith in them now. After taking off her hiking boots and socks, she rolled up the bottoms of her jeans.

As soon as her bare foot broke the surface, the black water transmogrified into a dazzling sheet of metallic blue. Laura cried out in wonder. Billy joined her, sloshing through the shallows. He sent a stone skimming into the darkness. It left a starry trail of blue, like the tail of a comet. As the ripples slowed, the water returned to its original oily black.

Minutes, or perhaps hours, went by. Laura wasn't cold. The sparkling water encased her bare legs like silk. 'What is this, Billy? Is it something from another realm, from your spirit world?'

'Nah, we're firmly on Planet Earth. Ever heard of bioluminescence?'

Laura smacked herself on the forehead. The creek glittered and shimmered like a spilled pot of metallic paint. 'How could I have been so slow on the uptake? It's what fireflies do – produce their own light.'

'Yep. Marine organisms like plankton and certain fish and jellyfish glow in the dark too.'

'So the fluorescent green crocodile . . .'

'. . . was covered in bioluminescent plankton,' Billy finished.

'That's why the saltie looked ordinary when they examined it in daylight. Wayne told us that it was covered in weed. So Supernatural Creek is not supernatural at all. It's just full of bioluminescent creatures.'

Laura waded from the water and sat down to put on her socks. 'Wait. There's something wrong with this picture. Why haven't the Jawoyn told anyone about this?'

He perched on a boulder. '*Because* there's something wrong with this picture. I saw the "piranha" that made the fisherman freak out. It freaked me out too. Because it wasn't from any river in Australia. Same story with the electric blue worms and headlamp fish. They're not from here either.'

Laura stared. 'Are you saying they've been brought here from somewhere else? Who would do that? More importantly, *why* would they do it?'

19

'**LAURA, IZZY! WAKE** up. Have you seen Elspeth?'

Laura emerged groggily from the cocoon of her sleeping bag. Paula was leaning into their tent. 'Elspeth? She's sharing a tent with, with . . .'

'Mia,' barked Paula. 'Yes, I know. So you haven't seen her?'

Izzy struggled upright. 'Why? What's happened?'

But Paula was gone. Izzy and Laura unzipped their sleeping bags in one motion, wriggled into their clothes and ran outside.

The sky was warship-grey. The air was charged. The creek had risen by more than a metre, suggesting that it was already raining hard elsewhere.

Mr Gillbert was even paler than usual. 'Let's not get ahead of ourselves. I'm sure Elspeth's close by. She'll be under a bush with a book and have forgotten the time.'

'It's 6.26 a.m.,' said Izzy. 'Not even Elspeth would be under a bush with a book before breakfast.'

The campsite was soon in uproar. A growing number of children were convinced she'd wandered too close to the creek and been eaten alive.

'There's this film called *Rogue* about a giant, marauding croc that terrorises a boatload of tourists,' said Lee. 'It's set right here in the Katherine Gorge. Maybe it's based on a true story.'

'Don't be daft,' said Jago. 'She's crying wolf. She'll be hiding somewhere, like Naomie and Merryn did when we were in the Macedon Ranges, waiting to see if we missed her. We should ask Captain Nipper to start the boat. She'll soon come running if she thinks she's going to be left behind.'

Aaliya looked doubtful. 'I'm not so sure. She wasn't a prankster. She was boring. Who goes on holiday and sits on the beach reading about missing kings and people being gobbled by crocodiles?'

'Don't talk about Elspeth in the past tense,' Laura said furiously. 'She's only just disappeared. What's wrong with all of you? Maybe if you'd spent more time being a friend to her she wouldn't have had to look for company in books. And she was the least boring person I've ever met.'

Aaliya was stung. 'What about you and Tariq? I didn't notice the two of you going out of your way to include her in anything.'

'Stop it!' cried Camilla. 'Stop bickering. That won't bring Elspeth back. We have to stay positive and help look for her. If anyone is to blame, it's me. I was always picking on her and making fun of her.'

'No, it's my fault.' Mia's face was tear-stained. 'We were sharing a tent. She got up to go to the bathroom at about three in the morning. I remember thinking that I should probably offer to go with her. But I was snug and sleepy and I couldn't be bothered. When I woke up, she was gone.'

Izzy put an arm around her. 'She'll be all right, Mia. She won't have gone far. A park ranger has arrived and Billy has gone to call some of his Jawoyn friends to help search. Hopefully, they'll find Espeth before the storm hits. It's coming in quicker than anyone thought. Mr Gillbert says that the Cicada Lodge has offered us their hotel as a shelter. With any luck, they'll feed us breakfast.'

'How can you even think about eating when Elspeth is missing?' Mia said sadly. 'If anything has happened to her, I'll never eat again.'

Paula came over and gave her a hug. 'Try not to worry, hon. We're doing everything we can. In the UK, the police often refuse to launch a missing persons enquiry until someone has been gone for twenty-four hours. That's because most children turn up within a couple of hours.'

Mia wiped her eyes. 'But we're not in the UK. We're in the Australian bush. Anything could have happened to her.'

'But it hasn't,' Paula insisted. 'Elspeth's choice of

books might be odd but she's a smart, sensible girl. Now think, Mia. What was she wearing when she left your tent?'

'Her pyjamas.' Another tear rolled down Mia's face. 'I teased her about them because I thought they were funny. The bottoms were purple with hearts on and the top had a picture of this dopey-looking kitten. She didn't say anything but I could tell she was hurt. Now I feel ill.'

'Now that's enough,' Paula said sternly. 'You are all to stop beating yourselves up. Nobody knew this would happen. However, it's a lesson to every one of us to be kind because anything can happen at any time. Not that it has . . .'

'Has anyone considered that Supernatural Creek might be responsible for Elspeth's disappearance?' said Jago. 'I don't mean because a croc ate her . . .'

'Jago!'

'Seriously, this place is the Bermuda Triangle of Australia. If it can crash a plane it can totally swallow a schoolgirl.'

At that very moment, there was a shout from the shore. Laura joined the stampede down the hill, the hot wind slapping at her face. Mr Gillbert tried to head them off but it was too late.

A ranger waded from the creek clutching a once white garment now chewed and bloodied. A sob escaped Laura as he held it up.

There was a kitten on the front.

20

LIGHTNING STUCK A pitchfork into the horizon as the white-faced children packed up their camping gear. They were returning to the Cicada Lodge by road. No one spoke. Nobody believed Jason Blythe when he begged them not to give up hope.

'Until we have concrete proof that Elspeth is no longer with us, the search will go on. In this heat it's easy to become dehydrated and disoriented. She could have blundered into a cave or gully and be lying injured. The Elspeth I know is a fighter. If anyone can become the heroine of their own survival story, it's her.'

The creek was a cappuccino torrent. Laura found it

inconceivable that she'd waded into it in complete darkness just a few hours previously. Had it really shimmered and sparkled a glorious metallic blue? She'd trusted Billy to keep her from harm, but now it seemed that something deadly had lurked in the water after all. Whatever had happened to Elspeth could so easily have happened to her.

Could. So. Easily. Have. Happened. To. Her.

BANG! Laura's brain lit up as if it was having a bioluminescent event of its own. She and Elspeth looked similar, especially in dim light. Laura couldn't see the resemblance but even Tariq agreed it was uncanny. Everyone assumed that a croc had snatched Elspeth, but what if a person was responsible? Perhaps the weird canoeist and/or Hawaiian shirt man? And what if Laura were the intended victim, not Elspeth?

In that scenario, the Straight As would go straight to the top of the suspect list. But what did they want and where would they take Elspeth?

Think, Laura. Think. There was a thread that connected everything. She could almost touch it but it remained tantalisingly out of reach.

'Laura, do you have a headache? Can I get you something? Let me help you. We're leaving any minute for the main camp.'

Paula patted her shoulder comfortingly. It was only then that Laura remembered she was supposed to be rolling up her sleeping bag and dismantling the tent. Izzy had already left in the first vehicle, too tearful to contribute to the packing.

The teaching assistant briskly unzipped and collapsed

the tent and set to work stuffing it into its holdall. 'Laura, I feel for you with all my heart. I wish I could turn back the clock to last night when we were all so happy. If there's anything I can do to make you feel better . . .'

'It would help if I could talk to Tariq.'

'Oh. Well, I'll tell him to come over, but I'm afraid you'll need to be brief. The ranger is keen to get everyone to the main camp before the storm hits.'

She gave Laura's shoulder a parting squeeze. 'Be brave, honey. Elspeth needs us to be strong for her.'

And just like that, Laura had her thread.

Honey was the link. Not the stuff she'd had on her toast for breakfast but the Honeycomb Conjecture, the mathematics puzzle in the Victorian beekeeping manual stolen by the Straight As.

'It took an apiarist to prove that the physics that govern the universe – gravity, symmetry, electromagnetism and nuclear force – can all be found in the humble honeycomb,' Mr Gillbert had said of TR Llewellyn. He'd described the hexagon as the world's 'most efficient structure'.

Laura had been nodding off by then but she did remember him saying that Llewellyn's research was later used by nuclear scientists developing uranium hex-something or other.

Nicco hurried past with his bags. 'Laura, do you need a hand? Our ride is leaving.'

'Thanks, I can manage. Hey, Nicco, have you heard of the name Padrino? Do you know if it's Italian?'

'I've never heard of anyone with a name like that, but it is an Italian word. It means godfather.'

Laura's blood ran cold. 'As in *The* Godfather?'

'*Sì*. Laura, we've got to go. What's this about?'

'Nothing. A quiz question. Thanks.'

Tariq came running up. 'Are you okay, Laura? Paula said you needed me. I'm in shock too but I refuse to give up on Elspeth. Roscoe and I wanted to stay and help search for her, but the teachers won't allow it. Everyone is leaving until after the storm.'

'Tariq, listen. We have an emergency situation.'

'You think I don't know that?'

'I'm not talking about the croc attack that never happened. This is about the Straight As.'

Tariq's face changed. 'Not now, Laura. Please.'

'They've kidnapped Elspeth, I'm ninety-nine per cent certain of it. They were after me but they've taken her by mistake. Tariq, we have to find her before they realise their mistake and try to get rid of her.'

'Whoah! Stop right there. Laura, I understand you're upset and you don't know what you're saying, but—'

'Tariq, we don't have time to argue. I'm begging you to trust me. When the Straight As broke into the bookshop in Paris, they weren't after *The Great Gatsby*, they were after the Victorian beekeeping manual. It contains the physics of Hex. That's this uranium compound that fuels nuclear weapons. Tariq, those monsters are here and we have to stop them. They're building a nuclear bomb.'

Her best friend wore an expression she didn't recognise. His words were a dash of icy water in her face. 'Laura, Elspeth's disappeared and you're making this all about you. Why are you being so selfish? I always thought I'd support you through anything, but you're on your own with this. You're obsessed. You need help. Our friend could be injured or dead and you're in some fantasy world where the Straight As are making atomic weapons in the Outback. I hate to say it, Laura, but I think you're losing it.'

'What's going on here?' demanded Jason Blythe. 'Tell me you're not having a row? Today of all days? I'm surprised at you. On the bus now, both of you.'

'Sorry, sir,' muttered Tariq. He strode off without a backward glance.

Laura didn't stir. Neither did the teacher.

'Laura, I understand you're devastated. We all are. But we need to pull together, not fall out or fall apart. How about I give you a lift back to the main camp? It'll just be me and some supplies in a Land Cruiser. Might give you some breathing space. I'll clear it with Paula and Mr Gillbert.'

Laura felt a rush of warmth towards him. 'Thanks, Mr Blythe. Yes, it would.'

'Wait for me by the ute – uh, the truck. Back in a jiff.'

A fat drop of rain splatted on to Laura's phone as she wrote a hasty text to her uncle.

URGENT!!! Elspeth's gone & SAs might have her. Follow uranium trail xx

There was no signal but she hit Send, hoping the message would wing its way to Calvin Redfern when there was one. She was shoving the phone into the side pocket of her rucksack when Jason returned.

'In the cab, quick! We're about to drown. Give me your rucksack, I'll put it under the tarpaulin with mine.'

Laura took one look at the wall of rain sweeping over the river and dived into the cab. The force of the storm and the thunder that accompanied it rocked the vehicle. It roared like a 747 at take-off. Jason had to wrestle his way into the driver's seat. He was already drenched.

The world beyond the windscreen was invisible. They could have been in a snowstorm. Laura was alarmed. 'Is it safe to drive?'

Jason turned on the ignition. 'If we stay here, we risk being trapped by flash flooding. Don't worry; I'll drive slowly unless the situation demands it. Like now. Hold tight.'

The Land Cruiser plunged forward. The wipers screeched as they strained to beat back the onslaught. Clutching the dashboard for added security, Laura never saw Tariq racing after their vehicle, frantically signalling for it to stop.

Jason Blythe, who did, accelerated. He watched in his rear-view mirror as Tariq vanished in the downpour. The fake teacher felt guilty but not guilty enough to stop.

Nor had he felt bad about smashing Laura's phone with a rock and tossing the pieces into a bush. His conscience rarely pained him. There was too much to play for.

When the danger of discovery had passed, he slowed.

Conditions were as treacherous as he'd ever seen them and he didn't want to have an accident. Not now. Not when victory was so close.

'You right, Laura?' he asked. 'You look tense.'

'I'll be okay when we get to the main camp. This is quite hairy.'

'Sorry. This isn't how holidays are meant to be, is it? Rain, missing girls, fights with friends. What were you and Tariq having a blue about?'

There was a long pause. The wipers squeaked back and forth.

'You'll laugh if I tell you.'

Jason smiled. 'Try me. I could do with some light relief.'

'Yes, but you'll think we're ridiculous. We were arguing about the Straight A gang.'

Jason Blythe looked sharply at her. 'The Straight As?'

'Uh-huh. Remember how, on our first day on St Kilda Beach, you told us off because we were in the café watching the news rather than playing in the sunshine?'

'Dimly . . . What about it?'

Laura didn't reply. She couldn't. As she spoke, Jason's words on that day returned to her with crystal clarity. The way he'd described Ed Lucas as the British Ned Kelly and predicted he'd never be caught. The admiration in his tone.

But it wasn't even that. The slip he'd made was using Lucas's middle name, a name familiar to only a handful of people. News-averse PE teachers were unlikely to be among them, especially when they pretended they could barely recall his famous codename. 'Mr X, Y, Z or whatever his name is,' Jason Blythe had said.

As the storm battered the Land Cruiser, the fake teacher's knuckles whitened on the wheel. 'What is it? What did I do wrong?'

He knew that she knew.

'You called him Ambrose.'

~ 21 ~

ED LUCAS HAD exchanged his wheelchair and widow's wig for the worn, dusty jeans and checked shirt of an Australian stockman. He'd also swapped the gleaming black Italian shoes he'd favoured as Deputy Prime Minister for scuffed brown RM Williams boots. No one in the Northern Territory would have looked twice at him. He blended in seamlessly. Even so, the smell of ill-gotten money that Laura knew so well still oozed from his pores, leaking out through his zesty new cologne.

'We really must stop meeting like this, Laura Marlin.'

'You know this monster?' cried Elspeth. She darted forward from an old sofa. Kim seized her wrist with one hand and tried to block Laura with the other, but Laura swerved around him and wrapped her friend in a hug.

'I'm so sorry, Elspeth. This is all my fault. It's me they want. You just got in the way.'

Ed Lucas shot his bodyguard a poisonous glare. 'That was Kim's error. We've had words.'

'It was dark,' Kim said sullenly. 'Small, blonde girls look the same.'

'Similar,' Laura and Elspeth responded together and burst out laughing. Given the gravity of their situation, it both surprised and strengthened them.

Then Laura remembered the bloodied kitten pyjamas. 'Elspeth, are you bitten or wounded?'

Kim smirked. 'A little trick with chopped liver. Not a scratch on her.' He released Elspeth's wrist with a warning look.

She rubbed it furiously. 'It was gross. I was trussed up like a Christmas turkey. There was nothing I could do to stop him ripping up the pyjama top my gran gave me for my birthday and smearing it with gore.'

The bodyguard frowned. 'First, we gave you a brand-new sweatshirt to replace it. You should be grateful.'

Ed Lucas cleared his throat. 'Diverting as this is, I'd appreciate it if I could get a word in edgeways. You're a welcome sight, Laura Marlin. When I was in solitary confinement in that grubby prison, the thought of doing battle once more with you and your esteemed uncle was about the only thing that kept me going. In this business, it's tough to find worthy adversaries. That's why I went into politics, in the hope of finding intellectual equals.

Boy, was I in for a shock! Nobody in government has the sense God gave a mushroom.'

He waved at the sofa. 'Sit, Laura. Let us catch up.'

They were in an underground office that could have belonged to the chief executive of any international bank. There was a teak desk, leather-backed chairs, a bookshelf and a gold-framed portrait on the wall. Two things set it apart. One was that it hummed with sophisticated electronics. The other was the atmosphere. It was charged with menace.

Laura did as Mr A had requested. There wasn't a lot of choice.

The door opened and in came Jason, sipping a cup of coffee. His smiley, not-the-brightest-light-in-the-harbour vibe gone. From the moment she'd guessed his secret, he was all business.

'How did you do it?' she asked Ed Lucas.

He settled back into his chair. 'Do you mean how did I escape from a maximum-security prison in a helicopter, fool everyone into thinking I was in Brazil and then turn up here at the thirteenth gorge, coincidentally the venue for your school trip? Come now, Laura. You're not the detective I think you are if you can't tell me.'

Laura glared at him. 'You used a drone to plan your prison break.'

He laughed gleefully, rubbing his hands together. 'Excellent. Go on.'

'The drone – probably a cheap one bought for cash from a toy shop – delivered messages through your cell window or to a prearranged corner of the yard. There was an article in the paper about how some prisoners are even getting pizzas delivered that way.'

'What a shame that didn't occur to me. Go on.'

'While that was going on, The Cipher hacked into the prison system and found out the dates and times you'd be in the prison yard.'

There was a startled silence. Mr A's eyes bulged from his fleshy face. 'Who told you about The Cipher?'

Jason cut in: 'More importantly, what do you know about him?'

'Only that he's one of the world's greatest hackers,' replied Laura. 'They say that in the Straight As, he's the power behind the throne.'

Jason choked on his coffee.

Mr A said icily: 'Do they now. By "they", I take it you mean *former* Chief Inspector Calvin Redfern? We'll see about that. Go on.'

'With the help of the drone, you organised a helicopter to pluck you out of the yard. It dropped you near a safe house. You'd have had a false passport and air ticket waiting, probably in the name of Mrs Padrino. You disguised yourself as an elderly female traveller in a wheelchair and flew to Australia. At the same time, The Cipher sent a Photoshopped shot of you to the newspapers, convincing them you were in Brazil. Did I leave anything out?'

'You left out all the fun parts!' cried Lucas. 'The genius was in the detail. The helicopter was unmarked and fitted with a radar-blocker. It dropped me in a field close to Wentworth Golf Club in Surrey. Hundreds of oligarchs and sports stars live around there. Helicopters come and go like buses. Nobody batted an eyelid when frail Widow Padrino was carried out of the chopper and into a waiting town car. Within the hour, I was at Heathrow Airport in my wheelchair, checking in for a flight to Darwin. The airline staff could not have been more helpful.'

Elspeth was gaping at them. 'I feel as if I've been parachuted into a chapter of *When Kings Go Missing*. This makes even the wildest conspiracy theory seem tame.'

Mr A preened. 'You ain't heard nothing yet.'

'The theft of *The Great Gatsby* was a red herring, wasn't it?' Laura said. 'All you really wanted was the beekeeping manual.'

Elspeth bounced off the sofa in outrage. 'Do you mean to say that I've been kidnapped, terrorised and had my pyjamas dunked in chopped liver because these brutes want to go into the honey business? Is it manuka honey? I've read that there are honey wars raging in New Zealand.'

Kim yanked her back down.

'It's not about the honey you eat,' Laura told her. 'It's about the Honeycomb Conjecture, a mathematics puzzle. The Victorian author of the book they stole was a physicist. The Straight As are using his theories to make nuclear energy fuelled by something called Hex.'

'Uranium hexafluoride if we're being precise,' added Mr A.

Jason laughed. 'If I didn't know better, I'd say these kids were after our job, Ambrose.'

Laura turned to Elspeth: 'They're planning to make an atomic bomb.'

Ed Lucas applauded. Each clap echoed around the

lamplit chamber like a pistol shot. 'Laura Marlin, you really have excelled yourself this time.'

'An atomic bomb?' Elspeth echoed faintly.

'Calm down, dear,' said Mr A. 'Your detective friend is good but she's not that good. Laura, I'm not a total monster. Uranium is nasty stuff. Not only does it destroy the environment, it's disrespectful to the Indigenous people who are custodians of this land. On the contrary, we're cleaning up the mine. Uranium is fiendishly difficult to dispose of but we're trying to make it environmentally friendly. I made a little money in the atomic weapon industry before the hazards of uranium became known. Now I'm making amends.'

'You expect me to believe that you broke out of jail and decided to celebrate your freedom by disposing of toxic waste out of the goodness of your heart?' scoffed Laura.

He chuckled. 'I might have done. It's not impossible.'

She'd rarely loathed him more. 'Yes, it is, because if you ever had a heart it was surgically removed decades ago. If you were innocently cleaning up you wouldn't have put bioluminescent creatures in Supernatural Creek.'

Jason was amazed. 'You figured that out?'

Laura kept her focus on Mr A. 'You wanted a distraction. When the Flying Doctor plane crashed and the newspapers were in a fever about UFOs and alien crocodiles, you must have been over the moon.'

Lucas rocked in his chair. 'I'll admit we were. What do you reckon, Jason? Should we confess the real reason we're here? It's not as if they're going to live to tell the tale.'

Laura reached for Elspeth's hand and held it tightly. The

other girl trembled with shock and fear, but you'd never have known it from the bold, confident way in which she addressed the room.

'A few months ago, I saw this documentary called *To Mars by A-Bomb*. Before you say anything, Laura, it's not a conspiracy theory. It's the true story of Project Orion, this top secret US mission to build a spaceship the size of a cruise ship and use thousands of mini nuclear bombs to propel it to Mars, Jupiter and Saturn. Their theory was that if you could blast a spacecraft into space at close to the speed of light, it would be possible to travel cheaply between planets.'

Jason and Mr A were not laughing now.

'My, but the pair of you make a formidable team,' remarked Lucas. 'Project Orion was shut down in the sixties, but the idea of using nuclear lightbulbs to put interstellar flight within our grasp is still being explored today by Deep Space Industries and similar companies.'

Laura's brain experienced another phosphorescent moment. 'Outer space! It all makes sense now. That's what you need the Hex for. You're not disposing of it; you're taking it some place where you can use it. You don't mind parting with a few million dollars if you're guaranteed a billion or two more.'

Jason watched her closely. 'And how do you propose we do that?'

'Asteroid mining. My uncle told me that one five-hundred-metre patch of asteroid could contain as much platinum as has been mined in the whole of human history. Asteroids contain gold and titanium too. Also, their ice can be made into rocket fuel.'

Ed Lucas's face was the colour of a bruised plum. 'Laura Marlin, has anyone ever told you that you're too clever for your own good?'

22

TARIQ DREAMED THAT he was being buried alive. The cold earth piled up on his chest, pressing down on him until he could hardly breathe.

'DON'T. MOVE,' instructed a voice.

'It's hard to move when you're being crushed,' Tariq murmured out loud. As he spoke, the nightmare loosened its grip. He surfaced with relief.

'I mean it, DON'T MOVE,' said Billy. 'Not even a millimetre. Don't open your eyes either. Don't breathe unless it's absolutely necessary. Keep your eyes shut and listen carefully. Your life depends on it.'

Billy, it seemed, was real. So was the weight on his chest.

Tariq stayed still but did what almost everyone does when told to keep their eyes closed because their life depends on it. He opened them.

Instantly, he squeezed them shut again, wishing that he could unsee what he'd seen.

He croaked: 'Tell me it's not . . . ?'

'A *Jurrang*? Some say *Jokplyn*. That means emu killer in Jawoyn. In your language, it's an eastern brown snake. After last night's storm, I guess it was looking for a dry spot to take a nap and thought your chest was the ideal spot. It's so happy it's smiling. Or is it? Maybe it's just licking its lips.'

Tariq didn't dare laugh or cry. Either could be fatal. 'What should I do?'

'Snakes don't bother you unless you bother them,' Billy said brightly.

'You know what's ironic? I've been telling everyone that for weeks. Turns out I was gravely mistaken.'

'No, you weren't. Just don't bother it.'

'For how long?'

Billy edged nearer. 'What do you mean?'

Tariq licked his lips. He was desperate for water. Though dawn was still pink in the sky he was sweating. 'How long am I going to have to be a mattress for a snake?'

'A minute, a day. Who knows? Maybe they're like cats and enjoy fourteen-hour sleeps. Trust me, it'll be worth the wait. One time I saw a *Jokplyn* bite a wallaby. Poor thing was dead in six minutes. The venom causes—'

'Convulsions, paralysis, kidney failure and cardiac arrest,' Tariq finished. 'I know. I've read about it. It's the second most deadly snake in the world. Billy, I can't lie here for hours knowing I could die at any moment. Can't you shout at it or wave a stick at it or something?'

'Nah, too risky. Eastern browns are cheeky. If it gets upset, it'll lash out at anything, me included. Not every bite carries venom but they tend to bite more than once.'

'So it's like Russian roulette?' Tariq said.

'What's that?'

'A stupid, deadly game. Gamblers put a bullet in a revolver, spin the cylinder and put it to their own head or someone else's. Then they pull the trigger, not knowing if they'll live or die.'

Billy took that in. 'Yep. That's how it'll go if I try to move the snake before it's ready to move on.'

Tariq opened his eyes. Yellow-brown coils and black-etched scales filled his vision. Mercifully, the head of the reptile was hidden from him but he could smell its dank, earthy smell. He was in a state beyond terror. He almost felt calm.

All he could see of Billy were his eyes and shock of black hair. The Jawoyn teenager was sitting under a tree. The lines on his forehead showed that he was a lot more concerned than he let on.

A tremor rolled through Tariq. Was this some form of karma? He'd been hateful to his best friend and now this?

From the second the cruel words had left his mouth, he'd regretted it. Even if he disagreed with her and even if he did think she was obsessing too much about the Straight As, there was a kinder way to say so. It was the least he owed her.

Laura and her uncle had saved his life so many times and in so many ways. Because of them he had foster parents who adored him. Because of them he had a home. He refused to let the whim of one snake take him away from her before he'd had a chance to say sorry.

He'd meditate; concentrate on slowing his heart rate. He'd do whatever it took to stay alive until he could see Laura again.

'Billy, my phone is in the side pocket of my rucksack. The battery's almost flat but if there's a signal, you could try calling the Flying Doctor. They'd at least have antivenom.'

'Good thinking. I'll take a look.'

But as Billy moved so did the snake. Its coils shifted on Tariq's chest and its head shot into view, neck bent into an S-shape. The warning hiss it blasted in Billy's direction sent an electric charge through Tariq's entire body.

For several long minutes neither of them dared speak. At last, the snake settled down. It showed no sign of slithering away.

'No worries,' said Billy, sounding as if he'd aged ten years. 'Be cool. Relax.'

'Like I have another option.'

There followed the most tedious hour of Tariq's life. Every time Billy attempted to sneak the phone from his rucksack, the snake's head popped up, twisting like a periscope. Still it showed no sign of slithering away.

Finally, Billy succeeded. He switched on the phone and waited. After two or three minutes, he groaned. 'Still no signal. Sorry, Tariq.'

'Thanks for trying.'

Tariq shut his eyes again. He was dog-tired after the worst night of his life. As the safari bus pulled out of Supernatural Creek, he'd begged Mr Gillbert to let him travel in the Land Cruiser with Jason Blythe and Laura because they'd had a row and he wanted to say sorry.

Touched by his concern, the teacher had agreed at once. They were still within sight of the Land Cruiser. Since Jason had smiled and lifted a hand, Mr Gillbert assumed he'd seen Tariq. The bus stopped to let him off, then roared away. The driver was keen to get the children to the safety of the camp before the storm broke.

But no sooner had the bus disappeared out of sight than the rain crossed the gorge like a cyclone. Tariq had almost been knocked off his feet. Half-blinded, he'd heard Jason's vehicle start to move. He'd yelled and run towards it but Jason hadn't seen him. In under a minute he'd been alone in the deluge.

Two thoughts had comforted him as he shivered beneath a rocky overhang, with night drawing in prematurely. One was that a ranger would return for him as soon as Mr Gillbert realised he wasn't with Jason and Laura. The second was that he had his rucksack with him. He had a dry change of clothes, his sleeping bag, a bottle of water and a packet of macadamia nuts.

As long as he stayed where he was and kept out of range of the fast-rising creek, he'd survive.

Another positive was that he had his phone with him. There was no signal but when the cloud cover lifted there might be.

When hours passed and nobody returned for him. Tariq

had wondered if a flash flood had closed the road to the main campsite. The bus driver had been worried about that. He'd finally fallen into an exhausted sleep and hadn't heard a thing until Billy woke him. Now, though, he was struck by a darker thought. What if Jason Blythe had seen him and had driven away on purpose? What if Laura had been right all along?

'Hey, what's this?' Billy was rummaging in Tariq's rucksack.

The snake's head shot up and twisted about angrily.

'Whatever it is you're doing, please stop,' whispered Tariq. 'You're upsetting our friend.'

'Why do you have an article about retirement funds?' Billy asked when the eastern brown had dozed off again. 'Are you planning ahead? Or did you keep it for the one about the UK Deputy PM skipping jail in a helicopter? Anyone could see he's a crook. He's as flash as a rat with a gold tooth.'

'Yes, he is,' agreed Tariq.

'Then why did you have it?'

'Long story.'

Billy grinned. 'We're on snake time now. That could be a minute or a day. Get your facts straight. The *Telegraph* hasn't. No wonder people don't trust journalists. The picture's been Photoshopped.'

'Impossible! It says in the paper that it had been checked by experts.'

Tariq was so agitated he almost forgot about the snake. It hissed with irritation and rearranged its coils.

'I'm guessing those experts haven't visited Australia. I'd

know that beach anywhere. It's near Darwin.'

'Billy, this is important. What makes you think it isn't Brazil?'

'Because I used to go there with my uncle. He'd fish and I'd hang out with my cousins under those three palms that lean together as if they're hugging. There's the boulder shaped like a camel and that's the driftwood I carved my name into.'

Tariq's mind whirred. He should never have dismissed Laura's gut feelings. Nor his own. He'd wanted so badly to believe that the Straight As were gone from their lives that he'd missed every sign that they were up to their old tricks.

If Laura was right about the Straight As being here, in the Katherine Gorge, she could be right about everything else. About Elspeth being abducted. About the uranium mine and their dastardly plans for it.

'This long story, it's connected to Laura, isn't it?' Billy said.

'Yes. It's also about Elspeth, the girl who disappeared. I think I know where she is.'

'When we get a signal, I could send an SMS to one of your teachers. How about Jason Blythe? He seems a good fella, a smart fella. He'd know what to do.'

All of a sudden Tariq remembered Jason's fingers darting like quicksilver across the keyboard of his laptop – the weird laptop he'd dismissed as a 'homemade cheapie'. He'd fixed up the blurred photo of Tariq and the water dragon in minutes.

Tariq recalled something else too: Paula remarking on how lucky it was that Mr Blythe had been able to join their tour at such short notice. The original teacher had been 'taken ill' or persuaded to quit.

'If I didn't have a snake on my chest, Billy, I'd bang my head against that tree. I've been an idiot. Laura is in a life or death situation. It's Mr Blythe. He's an imposter. You're going to have to run for help.'

Billy didn't move. 'Hate to remind you, mate, but *you're* in a life or death situation. I'm not leaving till the snake is gone, no matter how long that takes.'

'Then will you at least do me a favour?'

'What, babysitting you and the *Jokplyn* for – so far – two hours isn't enough?'

'Billy, I owe you my life, but this is not about me. It's about Laura and Elspeth.'

'No drama. Tell me what you need.'

'Jason's number is in my contacts. I put it there after he fixed a photo for me. Got it? Great. Forward it to Calvin Redfern and type this message. My phone will send it as soon as it picks up a signal.'

SOS. Laura kidnapped. Last seen with 'Jason Blythe'. The Cipher?

The clicking of keys stopped. 'What's The Cipher?' asked Billy.

'Not what, who. In England, we'd say he's the Power behind the Throne.'

23

'**DO YOU THINK** we really are too clever for our own good?'
Elspeth asked.

'No such thing,' Laura said at once. 'Grown-ups often
say that when they have a guilty conscience. If you know
in your heart that something is wrong, you have to fight
for what's right.'

'Even if it costs you your life?'

'We're not going to die,' said Laura. 'Tariq and I have
been in much worse situations than this.'

'Worse than being abducted and locked in a storeroom
at the bottom of a mine? Worse than being at the mercy of a
megalomaniac who's planning A-bomb trips to asteroids?

Worse than being told you're going to die at four p.m.?'

'Oh, much worse. In the Caribbean we were nearly boiled alive by volcanic lava.'

Elspeth eyed her with envy. 'Gosh, you're full of surprises, Laura Marlin. How on earth did you become such an expert on asteroid mining?'

Laura grinned. 'Wikipedia. And I'm hardly an expert.'

'But why were you studying asteroid mining in the first place? Aside from Camilla, who wants to be an astrophysicist, most girls I know are only interested in fashion, music and saving tigers.'

'You need to get out more,' said Laura. 'The world is full of incredible girls. The kind of girls who watch *To Mars by A-Bomb* in their spare time, for example.'

Elspeth grinned. 'Yes, but I'm just weird. So how do you know about asteroid mining?'

'It's a hobby of mine – researching obscure topics. You never know what might come in handy. I was reading about the Drake Equation, which was this attempt to calculate the probability of extraterrestrial civilisations in the Milky Way galaxy. I saw a link to an article on asteroid mining and clicked on it.'

Elspeth's eyes gleamed. 'Dr Drake was the founder of SETI, the Search for Extraterrestrial Intelligence Institute, as you probably already know. But did you also know that they've been receiving signals from comet 67P, an alien spaceship?'

She stopped when she saw Laura's expression. 'I didn't say I believe it. I read about it and thought it was interesting, that's all.'

'That's a relief.'

Elspeth picked at a square of stale lamington sponge cake, the Straight As' idea of a last supper. 'I'm confused.'

'About comet 67P?'

'No, Laura, about you. At school, you've always seemed kind of boring.'

'Thanks!'

'But then I worked out that it was an act.'

'An act?'

Elspeth nodded. 'Take last summer, for instance. You and Tariq had a dream job working as extras in a film in St Petersburg – a film starring your own husky. But according to you it was about as thrilling as a pensioners' bus tour of Bognor Regis. When you were reading out your essay on it I nearly slipped into a coma.'

Laura had a flashback to Russia. Mr A's meaty arm around her throat; his foul cologne filling her nostrils. She repressed a shudder.

'If this really is my last hour on earth, I'm not sure I want to spend it being insulted,' she said wryly. All the same, she knew Elspeth had a point. Under the Official Secrets Act, Laura and Tariq were banned from ever revealing details about their clashes with the Straight A gang. In trying to conceal their involvement, they'd evidently gone too far the other way. In future, Laura resolved to spice up her stories.

If they had a future.

The previous afternoon, Ed Lucas had taken her aside like a kindly benefactor, thanking her for being a worthy opponent. His habit of being excessively polite added a chilling and surreal dimension to their encounters.

'Tragically, all the best things come to an end,' he'd sighed. 'Our work at the mine is almost done. It's been going on for over a year, undetected by any intelligence agency. Tomorrow we're leaving for the last place on earth anyone would think of looking for us. All trace of our mission here will be obliterated. I have business to attend to between now and then so, if you'll forgive me, I'll say goodbye.'

'What are you going to do with us?' demanded Laura.

'Us? Oh, you mean you and your little friend? What a shame she got in the way. Can't be helped. Collateral damage is what we call it in our business.'

Laura wanted to fly at him in fury but she contained herself for Elspeth's sake. 'Please let her go. She knows nothing. She can't harm you.'

Mr A tapped his watch. He wasn't listening. Something in his eyes reminded Laura of another Australian expression: mad as a meat axe.

'Mmm, sorry, what was that?'

'Elspeth – will you let her go?' Laura asked desperately.

'Set her free? Gracious, no. A decade of planning has gone into Operation Final Frontier. And wouldn't you like a little company at the end?'

Laura did lose her temper then, but it was like railing at a statue. He stared impassively at his fingernails while she ranted and raved. Eventually, Kim silenced her with a wristlock.

'Laura, the sad truth is you've become a nuisance,' said Mr A. 'Tariq is almost as meddlesome and your uncle is a one-man wrecking ball. Fortunately, there's an easy solution. Losing his wife nearly finished him. When he learns that his beloved niece has gone missing at Supernatural Creek, probably ripped to shreds by the same croc that gobbled Elspeth, he'll trouble us no more.

'As for you and your little friend, at four p.m., Kim will light the dynamite that will destroy the mine and everything in it. I'm sorry it has to be this way, but at least it'll be quick. Goodbye, Laura.'

Laura found the courage to look him in the eye. 'If you get rid of me, you'll have my uncle to answer to. He'll hunt you to the ends of the earth and beyond. You'll never be able to enjoy your billions; you'll be too busy looking over your shoulder.'

'We'll see about that. We'll see,'

Laura didn't feel brave now. She was petrified. According to Elspeth's watch, it was three forty-five p.m. now. Fifteen minutes. That's all they had. Laura dredged her memory for the secrets of every locked room mystery she'd ever read. The body in the locked library/study/pub/living room was a favourite device of mystery novelists. But did anyone ever escape?

Think, Laura, think. What would Matt Walker do?

24

3.51 P.M. TICK TOCK. TICK TOCK.

'**CLEARLY YOU'VE BEEN** leading a double life all along, chasing gangsters and escaping from volcanoes,' Elspeth was saying. 'If I were you, I'd be shouting about it from the rooftops. So why don't you? Because you can't or because you won't?'

Laura managed a smile. 'A bit of both.'

'We're opposites, aren't we?'

'Yes, but we have complementary skills,' was Laura's diplomatic response. 'That's a good thing. Me and Tariq are the same way. He keeps me grounded when I go off on wild tangents. He's the bravest boy in the world. I was born suspicious, like my uncle, and Tariq reminds me that there are millions more kind, decent people than there are demons like Mr A. But sometimes I notice the stuff he misses because he's so busy seeing the best in everyone.'

Elspeth's face clouded. She looked as if she might burst into tears. 'I'm scared I'm going to die before I've had a chance to live, Laura. Before I've ever had a real friend. Until now, I've always preferred my cat and books to people.'

Laura put an arm around her. 'Apart from Tariq and my uncle, I feel the same way. My husky, Skye, is my soulmate. What's your cat's name?'

'Tiger. He's a ginger moggy rescue. I love my mum and dad and they love me, but they're in the middle of a hideous divorce. They're always at each other's throats. Tiger and my books make me feel not so alone.'

There was an ache in Laura's throat. All the time that she'd been making fun of Elspeth, Elspeth had been going through hell at home. When she'd most needed a friend, Laura had been cold to her. She'd imagined they were opposites but they were strangely similar. There'd been countless nights when she'd clung to Skye because she was feeling lonely and insecure, or missed the mum she'd never known. How would she cope if he was gone?

A tear spilled down Elspeth's cheek. 'I can't bear to think I'll never see Tiger again. He needs me. Who will take care of him when I'm gone?'

'You will see him again,' Laura said firmly, 'and I'll see Skye. Tariq or my uncle will work out where we were. They'll figure out a way to rescue us, you'll see.'

Her words fell flat in the small, stuffy storeroom. Jason had admitted to smashing up her phone. The chances that a signal had conveyed her text message to her uncle in the three-minute interval between her typing it and him destroying it were millions to one.

They already knew they could expect no help from their teachers or the park rangers. The fake teacher was so cunning that Laura was certain he'd have messaged Mr Gillbert with some excuse about how flooded roads had forced him to exit the park, taking Laura and Tariq with him. Perhaps he'd also claimed to have rescued Elspeth and be rushing her to hospital in Darwin.

It could be twenty-four hours before anyone realised they'd been snatched.

Seven minutes.

'I never thanked you for coming back for me,' Elspeth said. 'At least I won't die alone.'

'I was kidnapped,' Laura reminded her. 'I didn't have a lot of choice in the matter.'

'According to Jason Blythe, you were the only one who didn't believe I'd been taken by a croc. If you hadn't been so stubborn about that and if you hadn't fought with Tariq over the Straight As, you'd be with the others right now. You wouldn't be here with me, waiting to be blown to bits.'

Laura's heart juddered in her chest. Elspeth's words made the situation real. A shot of pure terror went through her.

'Unless there's a miracle, we have six minutes to live. *Six minutes.* It's such a waste. If I'd had a whole lifetime, I could have been useful. I could have been an archaeologist or an Egyptologist. I could have rescued more animals and made them feel loved.'

'You can't give up on your dreams and you definitely can't give up on Tiger,' said Laura. 'Think. Is there anything in any of your conspiracy theo— I mean, anything in *When Kings Go Missing* that might help us?'

'We couldn't boil an egg in the time we have left,' Elspeth said. Unexpectedly, she threw her arms around Laura and gave her a tight hug. 'If only we'd been friends sooner.'

Laura wished the same thing. 'We're friends now. That's all that matters.'

Running footsteps in the tunnel outside made them both jump. The last gang members were fleeing the mine. Elspeth shrank against the wall. She checked her watch. 'Oh, Laura, we only have five minutes left.'

'Focus on someone brave and strong who's inspired you. For me, it's Tariq and Uncle Calvin.'

Elspeth brightened. 'I do have one hero. Her name is Peta-Lynn Mann. I read about her in *Croc Attack*.'

'You're joking? This is the story you want to think about now, in what could be our final moments?'

'There's a happy ending.'

Laura smiled weakly. 'Go on then. I'm a big fan of happy endings.'

'About forty years ago . . .'

'*Forty*? You don't have anything more current?'

'If you interrupt, we won't get through the story,' Elspeth scolded. 'Peta-Lynn was twelve at the time. It was the Easter holidays and she and her mum and dad were staying at a campsite near Channel Point, this coastal reserve a couple of hundred miles south of Darwin. A family friend called Hilton Graham offered to take her on a wildlife-spotting expedition on his airboat. They were on their way back, close to the shore, when the boat wedged on a sandbank. As Hilton leaned overboard to grab the anchor, his revolver fell into the water.'

'Why was he carrying a revolver?' asked Laura.

'For protection. The water was shallow so he hopped out to get it. Out of nowhere, a four-metre crocodile launched itself at him and crushed Hilton's left arm with its massive jaws.'

Laura was aghast. 'Seriously, this is your way of comforting us in our final minutes?'

'Wait! It gets better. Peta-Lynn grabbed his other arm and clung on. There was a gruesome tug-of-war. Graham was screaming. Finally, the saltie let go. Problem was, they were still ten metres from the shore. They had no option but to climb out of the boat and try to make it to dry land. But the croc wasn't done and it attacked Hilton again. Can you imagine?'

'No.'

'Blood, spray and gnashing teeth,' Elspeth supplied helpfully. 'Throughout the ordeal, Peta-Lynn refused to let go of Hilton – even though she herself could have been prey at any second. She just kept dragging Hilton to the shore and the croc kept taking chunks out of him and trying to pull him underwater. What's incredible is she won. A twelve-year-old girl won against an animal with the highest bite force ever recorded – one ton per inch, the same as Tyrannosaurus Rex!'

Laura was riveted. Both girls were so caught up in the Australian girl's drama, they'd forgotten their own.

'By the time they got to their vehicle, Hilton was bleeding badly. Peta-Lynn patched up his wounds and radioed a nearby cattle ranch for help. She'd never driven before but she jumped behind the wheel and somehow drove for an hour through the bush until they met another vehicle coming to help. Hilton was rushed to Darwin hospital and his life was saved. Peta-Lynn won three bravery awards, including the Star of Courage.'

It took Laura a moment to return to reality. 'I now see I've been asking the wrong question all along. I've been trying to imagine what Matt Walker would do in our situation. What we should be asking is: "What would Peta-Lynn do?"'

And with that it was four p.m.

25

IT WAS AS if Laura's head was caught between two thunderclouds. The door exploded inwards. Jason Blythe tossed aside a sledgehammer and stepped through the wreckage. 'The cavalry's arrived but you'll have to bail in a hurry. Don't just sit there gawking like a pair of galahs. The detonator's set for four p.m.'

Elspeth found her voice first. 'It *is* four p.m.'

He yanked his phone from his pocket. 'It's three forty-eight. Your watch must be fast. Apologies for barging in. Ambrose has the storeroom key.'

'Is this another trap?' demanded Laura. 'Where are you taking us?'

'Just so you know, we have ten minutes to get out of here. Soon as Kim lights the dynamite, it's barbecue city.'

Elspeth squeaked with fright and ran to his side.

Laura didn't move. 'Ed Lucas doesn't know you're here, does he, Mr Blythe or whatever your name is? You're double-crossing him.'

Jason smirked. 'He'd do the same to me. He needs me. I don't need him. So why should I share what's mine by right? *My* skill, *my* hard work and he wants to pay me a tenth of what he's paying himself. I don't think so. Follow me. We're taking the tunnel on the left.'

Laura said in wonder: 'It's you, isn't it? *You're* The Cipher. You're the one who hacked into the prison computer system and organised the jailbreak. You faked the photo of Mr A on the beach in Brazil. And I guess it's no accident that the Katherine Gorge was on our school itinerary. How did you do it?'

'Laura, can we go?' panicked Elspeth. 'That's two minutes wasted.'

'Getting your class to the Katherine Gorge so that Ambrose could take revenge on you and Tariq was the easiest part of the whole operation. Believe it or not, I was a real teacher once. I know how schools work, what language to use, what boxes to tick. I hacked a few St Ives Primary email accounts, planted a few ideas, donated some money anonymously and watched the mayhem unfold.

'The only hitch came when Paula asked an agency to hire a local teacher to help escort you around Australia. We had to hastily arrange for a small accident to discourage him. A broken foot. Nothing serious.'

Elspeth stared at him. 'This whole thing was a set-up from the beginning? You brought twenty-eight kids across the world and broke an innocent teacher's foot just so the Straight As could take revenge against Laura?'

'And Tariq and Calvin Redfern,' Jason said matter-of-factly. 'It's a pity they're not here but our feeling was that if Laura died, that would hurt them enough. Between them, she and her buddies have cost our gang tens of millions and put most of our members in jail.'

A rumble shook the rock beneath their feet. 'It's make-your-mind-up time, girls. Coming?'

They rushed after him.

'If you hate us so much, why are you letting us go?' asked Laura as they ran. 'Why not leave us to die like Mr A planned?'

He waited until they'd reached the bottom of a shaft before answering. 'I got to know you. Worse, I got to like you. That was problematic for me. There's no guarantee that you'll survive even now. You're twelve kilometres and thirteen gorges from the main camp and it's wet enough to bog a duck out there. But my conscience will be clear. I'll know I did what I could. The rest is up to you.'

Elspeth glared at him. 'I suppose I should be grateful but I'm not.'

'You must have been a decent man once,' Laura said. 'What changed you?'

'No money in teaching and too many rules. I don't do rules. Then I got addicted to hacking. The rush of it; it's beautiful. No lock, no alarm system, no firewall can stop you. You're a living, breathing phantom.'

He gestured towards the rusting rungs on the shaft wall. 'You'd better go. The clock is ticking and I have my own life to save. It's not all fun and games, making billions. If it's any consolation, I wish I'd chosen teaching.'

26

'ANY CONSOLATION?' RAGED Elspeth as they started to climb. 'We're about to be blown into mincemeat and it's all about him. We're supposed to find comfort in the thought that, in a parallel universe, he might have been a good teacher. What a loser.'

Laura's admiration for Elspeth went up another notch. In dire situations rage, if channelled into action, was useful. Crying and feeling sorry for oneself was not.

The intense blue of the sky was a beacon of hope above. It gave her strength to keep hauling herself up. Elspeth followed more slowly.

'Don't worry,' Laura told her friend. 'It's only a matter

of time before Jason and the rest of the Straight As are behind bars.'

Behind bars, behind bars, went the echo.

'The Cipher will have years to reflect on why teaching would have been more rewarding in the long run.'

Teaching . . . more rewarding, more rewarding . . .

An explosion ripped through the mine, shooting choking dust up the shaft. The rung that Laura was reaching for broke away and spiralled into the gloom, narrowly missing Elspeth. Shards of falling granite peppered their faces. A whimper escaped Elspeth.

'Test every rung before you put weight on it but keep moving,' said Laura. 'Let's get this over with.'

Their leg muscles were on fire by the time they reached the top. Elspeth was a reader not an athlete and she was almost hyperventilating. The heat and dust didn't help.

'Laura, run. I'll catch you up.'

'Friends don't leave friends behind.'

They were at the back of the mine, hidden from view by a stack of green cylinders. Waiting for Elspeth to get her breath back, Laura spotted a ragged hole in the fence. It was well hidden by a cluster of shrubs.

A sonic boom ripped through the mine below. Fissures snaked across the red dirt. The cylinders juddered and stirred. For one petrifying moment, the girls thought they'd be crushed.

Laura grabbed Elspeth's hand and yanked her towards the window of wire. 'We have to go! NOW!'

As they scrambled through the gap and tore into the trees, they heard a lorry rev in the yard behind them. Their only hope of finding their way back to the main camp was to follow the Katherine Gorge, but getting to the river was like crossing a minefield. If some of the gang were escaping by boat, every step could be carrying the girls closer to disaster.

To Laura, murderous gangsters were the least of their worries. In a little over two hours the sun would set. They were twelve kilometres from the main camp. Laura didn't fancy their chances of navigating even one gorge in darkness. If Ed Lucas discovered that Jason had set them free, he'd go berserk. Those men loyal to him would hunt them down.

The river was a treacherous torrent, thick with debris from the storm. The sandstone cliffs were an angry orange. While Elspeth kept watch, Laura crept down to the jetty in the hope of finding an unattended boat. Even a kayak might save them. But there was nothing. Frantically, she tried to plot an escape route that wouldn't result in certain death.

In books, there was always a solution to these problems. A motorboat would be at the dock with the keys conveniently left in the ignition. Not this time. They were trapped.

The cliff on their right would have tested a mountaineer. The towering boulders to their left were interspersed with thorny brush and the kind of crevices snakes find appealing. Coils of black smoke rose from the mine. Swimming the river was not an option. It would be awash with saltwater crocs.

'We're in a pickle, aren't we?' said Elspeth, making

Laura jump by materialising at her side. 'If night falls and we're stuck here . . .'

She grabbed Laura's arm. 'What was that? Over there, by the reeds! A tail slid into the water. It looked too big to be a freshwater croc.'

'We'll be fine if we keep our heads,' said Laura with more conviction than she felt. 'We'll hide somewhere till morning. If the emergency services can't reach us, hopefully the Jawoyn people will.'

The rumble of vehicles had them darting for cover. A lorry and Land Cruiser were moving off down the road, spraying red mud.

Elspeth watched them go. 'It's so unfair. The Straight As have been getting away with murder for eons and they're about to do it again. They'll take their evil plans and toxic uranium and evaporate. No doubt they're off to destroy some other country's wilderness. By the time we're rescued, they'll be long gone.'

'Don't be so sure,' said Laura. 'Ed Lucas is smart but he's also a show-off. His ego will be his downfall. If he'd told park officials that he – or she, Mrs Padrino, the kindly widow – wanted to clean up the mine for the sake of the environment, no one would have been any the wiser. He'd have been praised to the skies. But it amuses him to turn his crimes into theatre. So he had his minions dump bioluminescent creatures in the water and carried out a controlled explosion so the tabloid would go wild over stories about UFOs and fluorescent crocodiles.'

'How well you know me, Laura Marlin.'

The girls clutched at each other in shock. Ed Lucas stepped from behind a sandstone pillar. Like a saltie sizing up its prey, he'd been there all along. In the deepening shadows, the army camouflage he wore concealed his body so well that his cruel, pale face seemed detached from the rest of him: a Joker's mask.

The girls edged backwards until they were teetering on the edge of the weatherworn jetty. The water was so high that it lapped at their shoes.

'Careful!' he said with a mirthless laugh. 'You wouldn't want to topple in. That *was* a saltwater croc you saw, Elspeth. Only a juvenile, though. There's a bigger one on the opposite bank.'

They couldn't help following his gaze. Fingers of shadow made the prehistoric creature near invisible. If it hadn't opened its mouth, Laura would have had trouble seeing it. But she had no difficulty making out its array of yellow teeth.

Mr A lifted a revolver and advanced a step. 'Looks as if you're caught between the devil and the deep blue sea, Laura Marlin. Which are you going to choose?'

'Not you,' said Laura, stepping in front of Elspeth to shield her. 'We'd rather take our chances with the croc.'

Behind her, Elspeth squeaked: 'Would we?'

Beyond a line of trees, just out of sight they heard hooting and banging and something not unlike a war cry. Laura seized on the diversion to murmur: 'Elspeth, was there anything in your *Croc Attack* book that'll help us if we have to swim?'

Elspeth gripped her arm. 'No way am I swimming. All

crocs have to do is glimpse you once and they have you in their sights like a sniper.'

'How is that helpful?' said Laura through gritted teeth. 'Can't we poke them in the eye or something? Surfers have survived shark attacks that way.'

'I have an idea,' said Ed Lucas, overhearing. 'You could try running across their backs the way James Bond did in *Live and Let Die*. Or rather, it was Ross Kananga who did the stunt. Bear in mind that estuarine crocodiles are apex predators which have spent two hundred million years perfecting their hunting technique.'

'Is that your motto: Live and Let Children Die?'

'No, Laura, it only applies to you and your unfortunate friend. Once again you have interfered ruinously with my plans, only this time you've gone a step further by influencing The Cipher, my right-hand man, to steal the keys to my kingdom.'

He gestured with the revolver. 'To prove that my heart has not been surgically removed, as you so poetically put it, I'm going to give you a chance, which is more than you deserve. Start swimming.'

Laura's blood froze in her veins. 'You wouldn't?'

'Oh, yes I would.'

Elspeth whispered: 'Laura, there's some drama unfolding at the mine.'

'You've only just noticed?'

'No, a sort of battle.'

In that instant Jason Blythe burst through the trees. As he sprinted towards them a javelin arced through the air. The skill of the thrower was Olympian. The spearhead pierced his shoulder with pinpoint accuracy, pinning him to the ground as if he were a bug.

'Get in the river,' yelled Mr A, rushing at the girls, gun in hand. 'If I'm going down, you're going with me.' He fired a shot at the ground to indicate that he was serious.

The girls leapt together. Laura popped up first, gasping at the cold and the strength of the current sucking at their limbs and weighing down their clothes. She stared around frantically. 'Elspeth! Elspeth!'

Across the river, the reeds gave a violent shake. Something was on the move.

Elspeth surfaced, coughing up water. Laura grabbed her hand and squeezed it. 'Stay close to me, Elspeth. We've got more chance together.'

There was a splash as Ed Lucas followed them in, gun held aloft. 'You swim across first, girls. Go, go, go.'

The monster croc slid off the bank with terrifying grace. Once in the river, it gave a flick of its great tail and slipped out of sight.

The girls trod water, flinching and squealing every time their legs were brushed by weeds or creatures unknown beneath the surface. Laura hoped the end would be quick and painless but she doubted it. 'Elspeth, what would Peta-Lynn do?'

'Well, there is one thing,' puffed Elspeth.

Around the river bend roared a speedboat. It hit a swell and took flight before smacking down beside Laura and Elspeth and surfing to a noisy halt.

Amid the confusion and spray, Laura had a snapshot of the Melbourne gardener, or maybe it was Hawaiian shirt man, only he was not balding and grey or wearing pink palm trees. He had clipped black hair and taut muscles and he was reaching down to haul Elspeth out of the water just as Tariq held a hand out for Laura.

As her feet left the water, she saw the croc streak below. On the boat, Tariq's hug held her up. He embraced Elspeth next before Billy, who was driving a ranger's speedboat, hugged them all.

The stranger came forward. 'Hi Laura. I'm Sam Lockhart, your unofficial and completely inept bodyguard. No doubt you recognise me. Your uncle hired me to take care of you and Tariq. I wish I could take credit for snatching you from the jaws of a saltie, but that is entirely down to Tariq's detective work and Billy's peerless boat skills.'

'That's not true,' Tariq said. 'If you hadn't chased away the snake, I'd still be there.'

Laura stared at him. 'Snake?'

'An eastern brown. Took a nap on my chest after Jason drove away and left me half-drowned in the storm.'

'I thought snakes didn't – oh, never mind. Sam, Ed Lucas was in the water behind us. He has a gun. Be careful. He's a lunatic.'

Elspeth pointed. 'He was right there.'

They all stared at the empty river. Laura remembered hearing that saltwater crocs were capable of hiding beneath the surface for an hour, waiting for their victims. Perhaps Mr A was the same.

They stood in silence for another ten minutes, watching for any sign of life. Finally, Billy started the engine. He steered the boat slowly between the rocks of the thirteenth gorge. The setting sun had turned the river blood-red. Close to the reeds, Laura thought she saw a movement, but the waves caused by their passing made it impossible to be sure.

She sat down beside her best friend. 'You took your time.'

Tariq grinned. 'Better late than never.'

~ 27 ~

'ARE YOU SITTING comfortably'

Laura nodded. She didn't trust herself to speak. She held her breath as Freya Ebury, proprietor of Wildwood Sanctuary, handed her a warm, wriggling bundle. The folds of the blue blanket parted. A joey peeked out.

'If you tuck him into the crook of your left arm, you can bottle-feed him with your right,' counselled Freya. 'Don't be discouraged if it takes him a few goes to get the hang of drinking. He's still getting used to taking formula milk from a human rather than his mum. Well, would you look at that! You're a natural.'

For several minutes, the only sound in Freya's living

room was the suckling of three hungry orphans: two wallabies and a kangaroo. Tariq was feeding the roo and Elspeth was playing mum to wallaby number two. Laura's joey was named Benjamin. As he drank, his dainty paws clung to her forefinger as if his life depended on it.

Both wallabies had lost their mothers in road traffic accidents. Greystoke, the roo, had narrowly escaped being a pet in a city flat.

'Why would anyone keep a kangaroo in an apartment?' marvelled Elspeth.

Freya took the empty milk bottle from her. 'You'd be surprised at how often it happens. Many people are incapable of thinking past the baby stage, even with their own children. They'll love a joey when it's mouse-sized, fluffy and cute but avoid looking ahead to the day when it's a hundred-kilogram buck as tall as they are. It's not going to be happy cooped up on a seventh-floor balcony. When that kangaroo can also kick like an MMA world champion and jump the length of a bus, it causes problems.'

Since the joey in Laura's arms was only interested in gazing up at her with worshipful brown eyes, she was in heaven.

So was Tariq. The stresses and strains of the past few days were forgotten as he plied Freya with questions about every aspect of joey care, right down to the formula of their feed.

When Benjamin had finished his bottle, the sanctuary owner showed Laura how to tip him into a pouch. The pouch was placed in a basket he shared with four other orphans. Freya put the lid on. 'Nap time,' she said with a smile.

Next it was the turn of the possums, rats and gliders to have dinner.

'Who wants to help me make a fruit salad for them?' asked Freya.

'I do!' volunteered Laura before realising that it entailed chopping up industrial quantities of honeydew melon, banana and mango into eighteen bowls.

While Tariq and Elspeth helped Freya's husband to deliver pellets and slices of butternut squash to the older roos, Laura and Freya carried possum takeout to various trees in the yard. One dish went to a boxful of silver and white gliders. The tiny marsupials were smaller than a newborn kitten yet they had no trouble flying between trees.

Afterwards, Elspeth settled into a hammock in the garden with Freya's copy of *The Lost Thing* by Shaun Tan.

'What, no more conspiracy theories or crocs on the rampage?' asked Laura.

Elspeth giggled. 'Turns out there's quite enough of those in the real world. From now on I'm going to escape into fiction.'

Laura squeezed on to the hammock. 'That's funny because I'm planning to read more real-life survival stories. Your croc attack book could have saved our lives. You said there was one thing we could do to get away from the saltie – if the boys hadn't raced to our rescue. What was it?'

Elspeth set down her book. 'It's a theory. I'm not sure if anyone has tried it and lived to tell the tale. Apparently, you dive deep at an angle. It's less risky than poking them in the eye – or so I'm told.'

'Compared to what – jumping out of plane with no parachute?' said Laura. 'I thought salties could swim at thirty kilometres an hour?'

'Yes, but they have to drop straight down like a submarine. Keep that in mind the next time you encounter one.'

Laura shuddered. 'Don't even joke about it.'

Elspeth took off her glasses and made a big deal of polishing them. 'Laura, I never thanked you for risking your life for me.'

'Yes, you did. I already told you, I was kidnapped. I didn't exactly—'

'I know what you told me but I also know that, if it weren't for you, I wouldn't be here. When Ed Lucas turned a gun on us, you stepped in front of me. In a life and death situation, your first instinct was to protect me. If that's not a true friend, I don't know what is.'

Laura gave her a hug. 'You'd have done the same for me. We were there for each other. No matter what happens, you have a friend for life. You, me and Tariq. The three of us are a team now.'

Elspeth smiled. 'You know what they say: two is company, three is a crowd.'

'Yes, but—'

'You and Tariq are a team and that's fine with me. But, hey, even the best detectives need back-up. If you ever need me, you can count on me.'

'And you can count on us.'

The setting sun was outlining the gum trees in gold when Laura went to find Tariq. He was sitting on a swing bench on the porch, admiring the didgeridoo Billy had given him.

'It's carved from a woollybutt tree. Billy spent almost the whole day making it while I was pinned beneath the snake. His plan was to use the vibration made by the didgeridoo to scare it off. He was almost done when Sam, the bodyguard we didn't know we had, showed up. Turns out he has a phobia about snakes. He whipped out his revolver and fired a shot into the ground. The eastern brown decided it was never going to get any peace with a person like that around so it took itself off to find a new bed.'

'Good thing too,' said Laura. 'I hate to think what would have happened to me and Elspeth if it hadn't slithered away when it did.'

'Or if Billy hadn't been brave enough to break the world record in his dad's speedboat,' added Tariq. 'Do you know it's never been done before? Nobody's ever been brave enough or crazy enough to drive a boat the length of the gorge. Too many hidden hazards. I think we only survived because we were mostly airborne.'

Laura sipped her guava juice. 'Hard to believe that St Ives Primary marketed this to us as the holiday of a lifetime. We should sue.'

Tariq snorted. 'Who – the school or the Straight As? This is all Jason "The Liar" Blythe's fault. If there's any justice, he'll be locked away for the rest of his natural life.'

There was a mischievous glint in Laura's eye. 'I take it you won't be signing any petitions for The Cipher to come to Cornwall any time soon? Such a shame. Hacking bank accounts would have been a fab addition to the curriculum.'

Tariq was embarrassed. 'Sorry for doubting you, Laura. It'll be a while before I live that down. You were right about everything.'

'No, I was wrong half the time and you were right the other half. For instance, it turns out that the Straight As had nothing to do with me being gassed in the bathroom at St George's. With everything that's been going on, Paula forgot to tell me that Mrs Brooksby phoned her, full of apologies. One of the tradies working at the school that day – a young apprentice – mixed up a couple of pipes and gas was leaked into the girls' bathroom. He only discovered it when he came up to fix a broken tap. When he saw me collapsed on the floor, he was afraid he'd get into trouble. He shut off the tap and ran to call his girlfriend, who worked in the kitchen. She rushed upstairs to help but by the time she got there Mrs Brooksby and Paula had already picked me up and carried me into the dorm. Needless to say, the tradie has been suspended.'

She shrugged. 'Still doesn't explain why there was a Joker on the mirror. And why my phone went missing and turned up under my bed.'

Tariq set aside the didgeridoo. 'That's weird about your phone. Maybe they wanted to check your messages. You should get your uncle to check it for bugs. By the way, I have a theory about the Joker on the mirror. The night we went to Mindil Beach, a group of us watched an Indigenous artist. He gave us each a piece of ochre and invited us to try it. Aaliyah drew what looked like a Joker.'

'A Joker? Why a Joker?'

'It was supposed to be a koala. She was annoyed I couldn't tell. They're her favourite animal and she says she doodles them everywhere. Maybe she doodled one on the mirror, not knowing it would show up when it was steamy.'

Laura wasn't convinced. 'I guess we'll never know. Personally, I think that Jason was behind it. It was a warning to me to back off. Maybe if he'd done a better Joker I'd have paid more attention.'

Tariq laughed. 'He'll have lots of time in prison to improve his art.'

A red truck bumped into the yard. Sam Lockhart jumped out and came over. He had such a distinctive way of walking and holding himself that Laura was annoyed to have been fooled by the private eye's cheesy disguises. There'd been three – the gardener at Blackwood, Hawaiian shirt man and the canoeist.

'It's your uncle's fault,' he'd confided to Laura the previous evening. 'He gave me no notice. As soon as he heard that Ed Lucas was on the run, he called me in Melbourne and told me to be at St George's within the hour to guard you and Tariq. I'm a private eye by trade. Nothing fancy. I track down small-time fraudsters and comfort wives who suspect their husbands of being unfaithful. Calvin sent me one blurry photo of you and some mug shots of the Straight As. Then he expected me to follow you around the wilds of Australia being Steve Irwin, Matt Walker and Jason Bourne combined. I nearly blew it on the first day when I mistook Elspeth for you.'

'But you did save me from being abducted by Kim at the market,' Laura consoled him. 'If I'd allowed him to "escort" me to the car park, I'm pretty sure I'd never have been seen again.'

He'd seemed relieved that he'd done something right.

Now he came up the path, looking sunburnt and weary. 'Hi kids, how's it going?'

Tariq grinned. 'Better. What's the latest on the Straight As?'

'The good news is that thanks to the quick thinking of the Jawoyn, all except one of the Straight As are either in custody or in hospital under police guard. That includes Jason Blythe, you'll be pleased to know.'

'Let me guess,' said Laura. 'Ed Lucas is still missing.'

'Yes, but as you know, the rangers set traps overnight in the thirteenth gorge. They found three salties, including one of seven metres. The chances of any human making it across that river alive are less than zero.'

'Why do I get the feeling that that isn't the bad news?' Tariq said.

Sam hesitated.

A hard, cold knot cramped Laura's stomach. 'They've found something, haven't they? Something that means he might have made it across.'

'I'm afraid so. Australian Special Forces found an empty

cooler box hidden in the bushes on the far riverbank. It looks as if it may have contained clothes and other survival items.'

'A passport?'

'That's what they're thinking but it'll be a while before they know for sure. Now, if you'll excuse me, I have some business to attend to before dinner. My guard duties will end when you're reunited with your group at Darwin airport tomorrow. Until then, enjoy Freya's sanctuary. Like you, she's on the side of the angels.'

Laura watched him walk away. His news had taken the edge off her happiness. As long as the fate of Mr A remained uncertain, she'd have to wear her detective spectacles twenty-four hours a day.

The phone loaned to her by Paula rang in her pocket. She snatched it out.

'Uncle Calvin! I've been desperate to talk to you.'

He laughed. 'And I you. I hear that my attempt to provide you with a bodyguard almost did more harm than good.'

Laura felt for Sam. 'He was there at the end, when it counted,' she said loyally.

He laughed. 'You do know that I'm a nervous wreck? Don't even think of asking me if you can go on any school trip or holiday ever again. The furthest you're venturing is St Erth. Tariq's foster parents feel the same.'

'The Garden of St Erth near Melbourne?' Laura said cheekily.

'No, not that one. The one ten minutes from our house. No, come to think of it even that's too far.'

'Why should Tariq and I have to suffer because Mr A broke out of prison and decided to try his hand at asteroid mining?'

'Oh, I'm not talking about the Straight As,' said her uncle. 'I'm talking about your dog. I've had to take a week off work to track him across the country. He's been all over the place searching for you. Don't worry. He's back safe and sound. He's tired and thin and still missing you but he's glad to be home.'

'I knew it! I knew something was wrong. I could just feel it in my bones. How could you lie to me like that? And don't tell me it was for my own good.'

'It was. Forgive me, Laura. I'll admit that we were economical with the truth, but in the beginning I was so sure that we would find him any minute. I didn't want your holiday ruined over a false alarm. As time went on, it became harder and harder to tell you. Give me credit for choosing to track down your missing husky over hunting Mr A. Given that you could have been blown to a pulp by that psychopath, I'm not sure I made the right decision.'

'Oh, you did,' Laura said. 'You definitely did. Skye's home and I survived. You're sure he's safe? How do I know that you're not just being economical with the truth?'

He laughed. 'I'll put the phone to his ear. Skye, say something to your mum.'

'Skye!' cried Laura, and the husky howled ecstatically.

When Laura hung up, a change had come over her. She felt lighter, more hopeful. She'd also come to a decision. Whether Mr A was dead or alive, she refused to live her life in fear.

If, in the future, she carried suspicion around with her like a cloak, she'd end up shutting out strangers and being afraid of the unknown. Her world would shrink. Darkness would swamp her, gradually eating up the light. Her spirit would weaken. One day she'd wake up and evil and hatred would have won.

It was far better to be the way Tariq was and try to see the best in everyone. She wanted to trust, not distrust; to reach out, not withdraw. She wanted to travel the world cuddling wallabies and watching fiery sunsets, even if those sunsets were eight minutes old. She wanted to light candles, eat cakes, walk her husky on Porthmeor Beach and fill number 28 Ocean View Terrace with joy.

Well, joy and the odd, scary Matt Walker book.

Tariq watched the emotions play out across his best friend's face. 'I've a feeling that it's all going to be okay, Laura. Everything.'

She smiled. 'Of course it is. And if it isn't, we'll deal with it. No drama.'

~ ACKNOWLEDGEMENTS ~

There is a persistent myth that writing is a solitary business and that finished novels are the result of an author spending months or years holed-up utterly alone in attics and sheds. The bit about the attics and sheds may be true, but the rest is not. Most books take a village and *The Secret of Supernatural Creek* was no exception.

To research it, I travelled to Melbourne, Victoria and Australian's wildly beautiful Katherine Gorge in the Northern Territory. Huge thanks to my lovely Aussi friends, Jane Kitto, Kellie, Carole and Don Santin and Nerrilee Weir for the travel tips, advice, droll humour and flat whites. I'm indebted to Willo, general wonder woman and the Top End's finest horse whisperer, for the whistle stop tour of Litchfield Park. I'm especially grateful for the introduction to Nina Keener and her incredible kangaroo sanctuary. Nina's Ark (www.ninasarksanctuary.com) was the inspiration for Freya's Wildwood sanctuary. Like Laura and Tariq, I got to bottle-feed a joey and it was quite magical.

Thanks to my ace support team: Jules for keeping me up to speed on the *New Scientist*, my mom for the Outback research, my Dad and sister, Lisa, for being there and believing in me, and to my friends for keeping me sane. I couldn't write a word without your love, patience and support.

I owe more than I can ever repay to Catherine Clarke, my agent. None of this would half as much fun without you.

Thanks also to my lovely Orion editors Helen Thomas and Lena McCauley for being so insightful, tirelessly enthusiastic and brutal with the red pen! Special thanks to Ruth Alltimes, Hillary Murray-Hill, Rebecca Logan, Jo Carpenter and Julia Sanderson.

There are those who say that you shouldn't judge a book by its cover, but I'd be delighted to have any one of my *White Giraffe* or Laura Marlin novels judged by David Dean's beautiful covers.

No book would be successful without the passionate, dedicated booksellers at Waterstones, Daunts, Foyles and fab indies such as Octavia's Book Shop, The St Ives Bookseller and Tales on Moon Lane. I'm so grateful to all of you.

Last but most certainly not least, thanks to the many readers who inspire me and make me smile daily. I especially wanted to thank the wonderful readers below. To them and anyone else who picks up *The Secret of Supernatural Creek,* keep reading and follow your dreams.

Lauren St John, London 2017

Roscoe Blanchard

Ava Byrne

Katie Winkless (and Pippin)

Rebecca Adelson

Athena Spitadakis

Emily Hoyle

Beth Lockhart

Olivia Judd

Molly Chapman

Ella Dickson

Blythe Taylor

Arabella Asamoah

Caitlyn Penney

Enya Rogers

Emilia Brooks

Holly Middleton

Anna Ledingham

Tanja Galetti

Hannah Henzell

Sian Mercer

Nicole Lasis

Katy Orchard

Georgia Friend

Hannah Newman

Leah Wilkins

Louisa Lilybell Atkinson

Christine Terblanche

Amy Tambini

Lauren St John grew up surrounded by horses and wild animals in Zimbabwe, the inspiration for her bestselling *White Giraffe* and *One Dollar Horse* series, as well as her acclaimed memoir, *Rainbow's End*. *Dead Man's Cove*, the first book in the *Laura Marlin Mystery* series, won the Blue Peter Book of the Year Award. She lives in London with her Bengal cat, Max.